Wednesday, February 19

Dear Diary,

or rather,

Dear Hermia in Thirty Years,

because I imagine that's who I'm really writing to, after all, in the hopes that someday I'll be able to pick this up, flip through it, and say, my heavens, what a delightful and perspicacious young lady I was, instead of having to imagine that I might once have been downright insufferable. Perhaps by then I'll even know what *perspicacious* means. (SAT word!) ☺ I know it's good, though, because Helena says it all the time (usually in this context: "Oh, Hermia, that's not very perspicacious of you"), and she knows what *everything* means. So, hi, future me!

Tui T. Sutherland

This Must Be Love

Based on

A MIDSUMMER NIGHT'S DREAM

by William Shakespeare

HARPERTROPHY®

An Imprint of HarperCollinsPublishers

This Must Be Love
Copyright © 2004 by Tui T. Sutherland

www.harperteen.com

Library of Congress Cataloging-in-Publication Data
Sutherland, Tui.
    This must be love / by Tui T. Sutherland.— 1st ed.
        p.   cm.
    "Based on A Midsummer Night's Dream by William
Shakespeare."
    Summary: Two good friends tell of strange occurrences between
themselves and the boys they like during a high school production
of "Romeo and Juliet," which are reminiscent of the magical
world of William Shakespeare's "A Midsummer Night's Dream."
    ISBN-10: 0-06-056477-6 — ISBN-13: 978-0-06-056477-3
    [1. Interpersonal relations—Fiction. 2. Theater—Fiction.
3. High schools—Fiction. 4. Schools—Fiction. 5. Shakespeare,
William, 1564–1616. Midsummer night's dream—Fiction.]
I. Title.
PZ7.S96694Th 2004   2003022305
[Fic]—dc22

Typography by Andrea Vandergrift
❖
First Harper Trophy edition, 2006

For Kari, my own personal Helena,
and Mum and Dad, for being so much cooler
than any Shakespearean parents!

—TTS

This Must Be Love

Dramatis Personae

HERMIA JACKSON, Helena's best friend, in love with Alex

HELENA NAPLES, Hermia's best friend, in love with Dmitri

ALEXANDER SANDERS, Hermia's best guy friend—and secret crush

DMITRI GILBERT, the (cute!) new guy

POLLY MASON, Athenwood High School Theater Technical Director and art teacher

THEO DUKE, Athenwood High School Theater Artistic Director and English teacher

ED JACKSON, father to Hermia

NICK WEAVER, the football team's star quarterback

PETER QUINCEY, Hermia's ex-boyfriend and a football player

LEO SUNG, a football player

FRANK FLUTIE, a football player

TOM O'KINTER, a football player

ROB TAYLOR, a football player

AARON REX, Broadway's hottest male star

TANYA MOON, Broadway's hottest female star

ROBIN, a key player in *The Faeries' Quarrel*

Other actors in *The Faeries' Quarrel*

Students at Athenwood High School

SCENES: Athenwood, New Jersey
Central Park, New York City

ACT I

February

AUDITIONS!! AUDITIONS!! — AUDITIONS!! —

THIS THURSDAY, 3 P.M.

Come audition for one of Shakespeare's greatest plays:

ROMEO AND JULIET!

Athenwood High School's Spring Production!

Football Players Strongly Encouraged!

- We'll work around your athletic schedule! •
- Plenty of parts that are short and easy to memorize! •
- Possibly some sword fighting involved! •
- Impress your friends! •
- Fulfills TWO elective requirements! •

For more information or copies of the script,
see Mr. Duke in the theater after school.

* Technical assistants also required; please contact
Ms. Mason in the art department if interested.

Hi Helena!

Period 2 geometry: BOOOOOOORING!

Wish you were here! Too bad you have to be all smart and stuff. ;)

Did you see Mr. Duke's sign? Hello, could you be more desperate? I know we need boys to try out, but football players? Is he serious? And who's going to react well to a sign like that? He has such a talent for insulting people right when he's trying to get something out of them. Remember when he wanted me to run that spotlight from inside the tower set in last year's "Spring Production!"? And he was like, "Hermia, I think you'd be really perfect for this job," and I was like, "Really? Me? Why?" and he said, "Well, your experience with the lights and talent for following the actors . . ." and I was like, "Wow, gee, thanks, Mr. Duke, I had no idea you'd noticed tha—" and he was like, "plus you're the only one short enough to fit in the crawl space. And remember [finger wag] I said to call me Theo!"

I mean REALLY. Yes, I'm short; do we have to bring it up all the time? I was nearly offended enough to say no, but then Polly asked me to do it, and she's the coolest teacher in the universe. (If my brilliant acting career somehow goes awry and I end up as an art teacher, I too shall wear overalls to school and carry a wrench wherever I go!)

Football players! *hee hee hee*

Ok, Mister Cranky is doing that suspicious-glare thing, so I better look more attentive. Oooh! Polygons! Does it *get* any more fascinating than this?

Let's see if I can remember how to fold this note in that elaborate way you showed me . . .

hugs
Hermia!

Dearest Hermia,

Well, it was a noble paper-folding effort, to be sure, although the end result is a little more pretzel-y than I think our dignified ancestors of yore would have intended. And if you're going to surreptitiously slip me a note in the hall, it might help the stealth aspect if you refrained from going "PSSST! HELENA! INCOMING!" as you fling it at me. But after all, living on the edge is what we do, right? We have to make our own danger, here in the riveting suburbs of New Jersey . . .

Anyway, yes, I did see the sign. It's quite appalling—Theo might possibly be the least subtle man in existence, I think. But seriously, what are the chances of any of those boys wanting to do theater—much less Shakespeare! It could only be worse if it were a musical. At least if they do audition, there's no chance he'll be casting any of them in big parts. Not after he actually gets to see them "act"! I'm sure he just wants to swell the ranks of the attendants at the court and in the sword-fighting scenes. Last year's almost all-girl production was a little embarrassing.

Maybe this will finally be your year! I mean, now that we're juniors, I think Theo should start casting you in the bigger roles. It's quite absurd that he hasn't noticed your shining talent yet. So maybe you'll get to be Juliet, and I can retire gracefully to the dressing room and spend my time designing costumes, which anyone can clearly see I am better suited for than these starring roles he keeps forcing me into. I would stop auditioning, really I would, but Shakespeare—it's too hard to resist! Besides, I seriously doubt he'll give me another lead. You'd be perfect for Juliet, anyway ... I mean, with the right costume, I'm certain you could look elegant and noble.

I wonder if the new boy will audition. Did you see him? I only caught a glimpse of him ... the principal brought him into my AP English class second period and introduced him, but then he got called down to the office again, perchance to fill out forms or something. He's a little insanely gorgeous. And check out the exotic, princely name: Dmitri! Isn't that splendid? Dmitri and Helena. I wonder if he is the soul mate I've been waiting for ...

Anyway, back to the fascinating dates and names of American history—see you at lunch!

Yours most yawnfully,
Helena

Hi Helena!

Yeah, right. Me as Juliet! I bet that's exactly what Mr. Duke is thinking (sorry; I still can't bring myself to call him Theo—it's too weird, especially since it's Theo in the theater and Mr. Duke in English class—I just know I'll forget and get it wrong and end up in trouble, so it's safer this way!). I bet he's all, *Hmm, let's see, I have this completely perfect, beautiful blond girl who speaks Shakespeare like she was born to do so, but instead I think I'll cast her ridiculously short, frenetic, chubby little friend who so far has been running lights and playing courtesans or trees, because ha-ha! that'll surprise people! And surprising people is what I do! Let me just toss my decades-long history of typecasting straight out the window!* I bet that's EXACTLY what's going on in his head. ☺

But that's ok. Juliet's not really my kind of part anyway. Blah blah love, swoon, melt, expire, plus, like, how dumb do you have to be not to have a backup way of getting the message to Romeo? And who would *want* a guy that jumps to conclusions and does idiot things like kill himself without checking first to see if you're really truly dead? And aren't they only, like, fourteen or something? I mean, I was a ditzy fourteen-year-old, but even *I* knew better than to think *those* relationships were going to last. Fourteen-year-old boys are *morons*. Not that sixteen- and seventeen-year-old boys are much better.

Ok, except maybe Alex. Helena, it's driving me crazy! He's so sweet and perfect sometimes, but I can't even tell if he likes me, you know, *that* way. I'm worried that we've been friends for too long, and now we can't ever cross that magic boundary line into being *more*. But that doesn't seem fair. How was I to know two years ago that he would be so perfect for me? And I was dating that other guy then (Bart? Was it Bart? Or was it Rob? Maybe it was Bart, then Rob. Or maybe that's when I was kind of dating both of them, because Bart was cute and mopey and hard to break up with, but Rob had a car and brought me flowers. Hrmm . . .), and Alex seemed like such a perfect friend that it didn't even occur to me that he'd be great dating material as well.

So I was dumb! I was fourteen! Now I'm SIXTEEN and I'm SO much more mature and I've figured out how perfect and wonderful Alex is, and surely it can't be too late, can it? Plus he's had plenty of opportunities to ask me out in the last two years. I was single for at least three weeks between Rob and Ken, and I swear there was like a MONTH between Ken and Trent, and maybe not so much between Trent and Chad, but after Chad there was that whole week where I was super-depressed and spent all that time crying on Alex's shoulder and at NO point did he make anything that could be even remotely construed as a move on me (hasn't he seen *When Harry Met Sally*? Doesn't he know how to cheer a girl up?), and maybe if he HAD, we wouldn't have had that whole six-month fiasco with Pete (speaking of goober football players!) and in any case *now* I've been single for THREE WHOLE MONTHS *and* I've dropped *plenty* of hints, but nothing! Zip! No reaction! What am I supposed to do?

I would ask *him* out, but then, what if he gives me that "I don't want to ruin the friendship" speech, which, by the way, is, like, the most effective way *to* ruin the friendship, as far as I'm concerned. It didn't work in eighth grade when you gave it to Nick Weaver, or in sixth when I gave it to Paul Trumbull, and I really don't even want to risk going there. You know? Yeeeesh.

Oh, SIGH. I should stop thinking about this. Especially since I just missed *everything* Miz Harpy said about what's going to be on Friday's history test. ARRRGH, why why why do you have to be in all these smart classes now, so I can't even study off your notes anymore?

On the plus side, Alex looked like he was paying attention all period, so maybe I can get the notes from him. And then he can make some unbelievably cute joke about what a slacker I am, and ha-ha, what was I thinking about if not the Mexican-American War? and I can be like, oh, I don't know, certainly not YOU, no, no sir, absolutely not. And then maybe we'll study together tonight and make pasta with his mom and joke about terrible TV shows and this whole thrilling dance of *not* dating can just go on and on and on.

Not that I'm pining, mind you. But he is SO adorable!

See you in PE—ugh, more running in circles . . .

hugs
Hermia!

P.S. You want to criticize MY note-passing procedures? How many times have I told you not to put notes in my locker? Or when you do, make sure they're shoved firmly into the little slats so they'll stay put. You know I can't find ANYTHING in there! When you told me at lunch that you'd left me a note, I had to spend like fifteen minutes digging through the mess before I found it. Come on, secret agent girl—you have to account for the very slight flaws of your secret agent partner here!

P.P.S. That new boy you pointed out in the cafeteria hasn't popped up in any of my classes yet—he's probably all smart-like and is taking AP classes, like you. Well, hey, if he *is* this soul mate you've been waiting for for like forever, I say: ABOUT FLIPPIN' TIME! ☺

P.P.P.S. I'm going to talk to Polly after school about the set design she's working on. Want to join me?

Hermia—Guess what?! Dmitri is in all *my afternoon classes, apart from PE! Isn't that the most marvelous coincidence? This has* destiny *written all over it. And he is even more gorgeous up close, or at least the back of his head is, which I had the opportunity to gaze upon at length during calculus, because Mr. Keener sat him right in front of me! Oh please please let him be a theater person ... Can you imagine how romantic it would be if he were Romeo and I were Juliet? Theo could be an instrument of fate here, and he doesn't even realize it!*
Helena

P.S. Incidentally, I wonder if your astonishing string of terrible boyfriends who don't even remotely deserve you has anything to do with their monosyllabic names. Perhaps you should try someone with a few more syllables ... and yes, Alexander qualifies. Although it's not quite as romantic sounding as Dmitri, of course ... I know my soul mate will have a noble-sounding name like that ... or perhaps precisely *that, happy dreamy sigh ...*

P.P.S. You are NOT chubby! You're curvy! And surely Theo will break the mold and surprise us one day, don't you think? You are so talented, it's simply unjust.

P.P.P.S. I hardly see how it could be construed as my *fault that your locker is such a disastrous mess.*

P.P.P.P.S. Sure—I'll meet you at the art studio at 3:15, and we can talk to Ms. Mason then, ok?

Date: Tuesday 18 February 21:45:00
From: AmazonGrrrl! [HermiaJ@athenwood.edu]
To: Poetess [HelenaN@athenwood.edu]
Subject: Dads suck

hey chica!

BLEH. I would totally call you on the phone, like a regular person, but Dad had a major crazy fit today, so I'm not allowed to call ANYBODY, allegedly for the rest of the week, but I think he'll forget by tomorrow. And it's so not even my fault! Apparently Mom called today, while I was with you and Polly after school, and she wanted to know where I was, and even though Dad hardly *ever* pays attention to where I am AND I had even LEFT HIM A MESSAGE saying I'd be staying late to do theater stuff and then going to Alex's for dinner and studying (a message he apparently didn't get because he still hasn't figured out how to check our new voice-mail system at home, which, hi, is totally not my fault) he completely wigged out because it made him look like a bad father or something in front of his ex, so I'm phone-grounded for the rest of the week.

Which is better than being really grounded, since ha-ha! I can still use e-mail! I'm so fiendish! Lucky Dad likes Mr. Duke so much, because it means I can always use theater as a super-excellent reason why I can't be grounded ("But Dad! Mr. Duke NEEDS me to crawl inside a tiny, rickety, plywood tower-like construction to shove a giant heavy scalding spotlight around!"). Too bad Dad didn't go to college with *all* of my teachers . . .

Oh! Eek! You're on-line! I'm going to send this and go IM you right now . . .

AmazonGrrrl!: Boo!

Poetess: Hey, sunshine. I might have known you'd be on. Hang on while I read your e-mail . . .

AmazonGrrrl!: It's not that interesting. Just Dad being a freak because of Mom again. You'd think no one had ever left a guy for a woman before!! ;)

Poetess: Nine years later, and he's still obsessing? Your father could clearly benefit from attempting the dating scene again.

AmazonGrrrl!: Ew, ok, things I SERIOUSLY don't want to think about. Besides, like you should talk, Miss I-Refuse-to-Date-Until-I-Find-the-Absolute-Completely-Perfect-Man-for-Me.

Poetess: As I believe I have made abundantly clear, I think it's a little absurd to date someone whom you're inevitably going to break up with anyway. When I fall in love, it's going to mean something, and until then, I don't see why I should waste my time with high school boys who can't even spell Byron, let alone quote him.

AmazonGrrrl!: Yeah yeah, I know. Soooo . . . do you think this new boy is a Byron-quoter?

Poetess: Oh, I hope so! He looks like he *should* be . . . with his soulful brown eyes . . . and the slightly long but perfectly coiffed poet's hair . . .

AmazonGrrrl!: I'm not into blonds, personally. Except you, of course. ☺

Poetess: He's not just a BLOND, Hermia. His golden locks are an outward manifestation of his noble lion's heart.

AmazonGrrrl!: Oh, my. How could I possibly have missed that! But ok, I will admit that from across the cafeteria, he does look utterly—erm—Byronesque.

Poetess: I think we're destined for each other. Don't you? I mean, could it really be mere *coincidence* that we have five out of eight classes together? I hardly think so!

AmazonGrrrl!: Inconceivable!

Poetess: I'm sure that once he's a little more settled in, he'll have time to look around and then he'll clearly spot me and how kindred our spirits are, and it'll be simply magical.

AmazonGrrrl!: Like, hey, soul mates ahoy!

Poetess: Well, ok, only more romantic, you nonsense person.

Poetess: Oh! And by the way! I can't BELIEVE you brought up that Nick Weaver catastrophe in your note today!

AmazonGrrrl!: *hee hee hee!*

Poetess: That was three years ago! And he still hasn't spoken to me since then, except, you know, really awkwardly in the hall sometimes. I think he hates me. Did I ever tell you Chrissy Canton once heard him call me a stuck-up snob?

AmazonGrrrl!: Hmm, let's see . . . only about A THOUSAND TIMES.

Poetess: Me! A stuck-up snob! As you are well aware, Hermia, I make a concerted effort to socialize in a sincerely interested fashion with all manner of people, so as to distinguish myself from my absurdly haughty father, who is the very epitome of stuck-up snobdom.

AmazonGrrrl!: Right—Mr. Ooh-La-La Naples! Although, you know, if I had more money than the entire rest of Athenwood combined, and I were distantly related to the monarchy of several European countries, I probably wouldn't want to hang out with regular Athenwood lugs like my dad either.
P.S. "Snobdom" is my new favorite word.

Poetess: It's *one* European country, and *very* distantly related, and *not* that much money. In any case, do you not agree that it is shallow of Nick to accuse me of being a stuck-up snob based upon the mere fact of my family being the richest in town? I hardly think I should be thus harshly judged for circumstances so utterly beyond my control.

AmazonGrrrl!: Maybe he was just upset about how you rejected him. You know how those football guys talk when they're around each other, all rah-rah and bluster and

I'm-so-tough. I'm sure he didn't mean it. (Why do I feel like we've had this conversation before . . . oh, BECAUSE WE HAVE.)

Poetess: Well, I'm sorry, but I do think it was rather unfair of him. I tried to turn him down nicely. He obviously couldn't comprehend how complicated romance can be, whereas I could clearly foresee all the possible inevitably disastrous conclusions, despite being only thirteen.

AmazonGrrrl!: Hmm. Incidentally, I don't know that I'd trust Chrissy's word completely on this. Haven't you noticed how she looooooooooooves to gossip? Maybe she was making it up to cause trouble.

Poetess: That seems highly unlikely. Why would someone do that?

AmazonGrrrl!: Have you ever thought about, I don't know, ASKING him if it's true?

Poetess: Certainly not! He's far too high and mighty nowadays to deign to speak to the likes of me.

AmazonGrrrl!: That poor guy.

Poetess: Right. Poor super-popular star quarterback Nick. That's a perfect example of my theory, by the way: if we *had* dated, he would clearly have ditched me by now to be a big-shot football jock who spends all his time with bubbleheaded cheerleaders.

AmazonGrrrl!: Do you think so? He seemed so nice, at least whenever we all hung out in elementary school. He was always bringing you things like cute erasers and parts of Transformers. ☺

Poetess: I can't believe you remember that! I never really quite grasped the underlying meaning of that Transformer parts thing.

AmazonGrrrl!: And he seems like the one guy on the football team who *hasn't* dated any of the cheerleaders. Unlike, say, PETE, who has dated ALL of them, several while I was going out with him, the rat bastard.

Poetess: Ok, but weren't you secretly falling in love with Alex that whole time anyway?

AmazonGrrrl!: *SIIIIIIIIIIIIIIIIIIIIIIIIIIIIIIIIIIIIIIIIGH*

Poetess: How was the study session tonight?

AmazonGrrrl!: Same as ever. *sigh*

Poetess: I'm confident that he'll come to his senses soon. How could he not be secretly in love with you? He spends almost every waking minute with you, except for the times I've claimed you all for myself, of course. ☺ And he never seems interested in other girls.

AmazonGrrrl!: He never seems interested in me, either! ARGH!

AmazonGrrrl!: Anyway, blah blah my tragic love life. At least I'm going to ACE the history test on Friday!

Poetess: Really? I thought you hated the whole Manifest Destiny era.

AmazonGrrrl!: I do! But Alex helped me memorize the details really well. I wish someone could explain to me why we require TWO YEARS of this American history nonsense. I mean, hello, we only get one year of European history, which includes like fifty countries and like thousands of years, whereas American history is ONE country and like TWO HUNDRED years. Blah blah BLAH!

Poetess: I fervently agree, Hermia, but that reminds me of my own American history homework, or more specifically, of how I haven't exactly started it yet. I should probably get going.

AmazonGrrrl!: No problem. I'm going to go reread *Romeo and Juliet*, memorize some of Juliet's lines, laugh at how dismally unlikely it is that Mr. Duke will ever cast me as her, and then flip through to see if there are any courtesans in it. Or trees. ;)

Poetess: I'll keep my fingers crossed for you! Good night, good night. Parting is such sweet sorrow, that I shall say "good night" till it be morrow!

AmazonGrrrl!: See, that's what I'm talking about. Like anyone else has a chance with you around! ☺ Good night to you, too! Sweet dreams of fancy-name new boy!

Date: Tuesday 18 February 23:16:00
From: Poetess [HelenaN@athenwood.edu]
To: AmazonGrrrl! [HermiaJ@athenwood.edu]
Subject: Don't forget!

Yes, I know, I'm going to bed this minute, but I wanted to remind you about the diary thing we talked about. Remember? Trust me, it's a good idea. I love my journal—it's the best vehicle for expression you could possibly imagine. Not to mention I will be mortally offended if you don't avail yourself of my carefully considered birthday gift—it took me *weeks* to find a blank book for you that had tigers on it instead of flowers! ☺

Helena

Wednesday, February 19

Dear Diary,
> **or rather,**
>> **Dear Hermia in Thirty Years,**

because I imagine that's who I'm really writing to, after all, in the hopes that someday I'll be able to pick this up, flip through it, and say, my heavens, what a delightful and perspicacious young lady I was, instead of having to imagine that I might once have been downright insufferable. Perhaps by then I'll even know what *perspicacious* means. (SAT word!) ☺ I know it's good, though, because Helena says it all the time (usually in this context: "Oh, Hermia, that's not very perspicacious of you"), and she knows what *everything* means. So, hi, future me! Welcome back! (And hey,

congratulations on finding this thing again—if the condition of my future mansions is anything like the current state of my locker!)

I was thinking about all the different ways to start a book. I mean, I figure one day I'm going to be wildly famous, and they'll probably want to publish this Very First Diary of Hermia for posterity, don't you think? So it should have some sort of lofty, fascinating beginning that expresses the underlying themes of my life in a concise, deeply metaphoric way, but for pete's sake, that's what Helena is good at, not me! I don't think my life HAS themes. Except maybe "I love Alex, la la la, when is he going to notice, la la la, why are boys dense, la la SIGH." (Ok, perhaps "la la la" isn't a theme, per se. Maybe it's more of a MOTIF. *hee hee* I am SO paying attention, English teachers!)

Anyway. So instead of doing all that important-sounding business, I think it would be much more helpful if I jumped straight into describing the Most Important Characters. I mean, I know *most* good books begin mid-conversation, as we join a story in progress, but I do think that for *my* story it is *important* to know the cast first, or else you'll be like "who?"— or, even worse, you'll get them all confused and think Dmitri and Alexander are the same person which is SO clearly not the case, because Alex is the light of my life (even if he doesn't know it yet), handsome, rebellious, and charming, whereas Dmitri may be a mere (boring) footnote in our riveting lives. ☺

Also, I certainly wouldn't want anyone calling Helena "Hermia" by accident or thinking I'm her because *I* am the ONLY Hermia and that's all there is to it. (Also, I do not pine, and I am not fond of lavender OR skirts, so I do not see how anyone *could* get us confused anyhow.)

So. To begin: my best friend, Helena. Helena is tall and amazingly beautiful. She's always been the tallest girl in our class, and when they say clothes look better on tall people, they're talking about people like Helena. She's got this long, straight, blond-gold hair and large gray-green eyes and perfect posture, and it's a good thing I like her so much or I wouldn't be able to stand her.

People always say we're equally pretty "in different ways," by which they mean *she* is beautiful and *I* am "cute." That's just the way it is. Brown eyes + outrageously curly brown hair + short = cute. But fortunately I've had a long time to get over that, because we've been best friends since we were four.

We met on the first day of kindergarten, when she gave me a cupcake and I gave her a salamander in return, and she screamed and dropped it and we had to overturn the whole classroom to catch it and release it back into the pond. I suppose Helena was expecting something a bit more sedate, like a cookie.

You might think this would be an inauspicious beginning to our lifelong friendship, but I knew right then that there was something different about her. Maybe it was the way that she laughed, instead of crying for a week straight like some of the other wimpy girls (AND boys) in the class did. But Helena started laughing and laughing, and she has this fully magical,

21

enchanted, wholehearted laugh that makes you want to believe in fairies and stuff like that. She acts like she's all serious and soulful most of the time, which is why making her laugh is so much fun, because I know underneath she's as crazy as I am.

So I'm way over the height/prettiness thing. Some people think I have some sort of complex about my height, but it's so not true. I never think about it. Hardly ever. Nobody even notices that I'm short, not really. *Alex* doesn't notice, anyhow.

Alex moved to Athenwood when we were all about fourteen. He used to go to a snooty private school a few towns over, but the family moved here because Athenwood was the next best school in the area after the last one expelled him for doing something shocking! like talking back to a teacher.(!)

Oh, fine, and there might have been a fistfight with another student involved. Alex assures me the other guy definitely had it coming (something about lifelong competition, a race, and a mysterious profusion of hermit crabs in someone's running shoes), and he's probably right; I'm certainly happy he's here, in any case. He has twinkly brown eyes and messy brown hair and the best smile ever and if I don't stop this RIGHT NOW I really am going to turn into silly soulful Helena.

Hmmmmm.

Ok, maybe just one example of how perfect he is. ☺ His first day at our school, he "accidentally" set fire to a hanging wall chart in earth sciences, and in the ensuing confusion he somehow managed to set all the animals in our terrarium free, which I'd been planning on doing myself. Isn't that amazing? I had a feeling we'd be really good friends then—although I somehow managed to miss the obvious fact of what a perfect boyfriend he would be, too. ARGH. You know, there should be guardian angels for relationships. They could swoop down and bop you on the head whenever you do something dumb, like assuming Alex is just friend material, or thinking that dating Pete Quincey is a GOOD idea.

Then there's Dmitri. He's Helena's DREAMBOAT perfect guy, although goodness knows how she can tell, since they haven't even spoken to each other yet. *I* am dubious about him because he hasn't said hi to me *or* Helena yet, even when we pass him in the halls and I wave vigorously (while Helena looks mortified). Plus he seems really full of himself, I think. You know those guys who always seem hyper-aware of how they're standing, what they're wearing, and how many people are looking at them? He totally seems like one of those. But then, I guess I'm not looking with Helena's eyes, and she probably doesn't understand what I see in Alex, either. (There, wasn't that mature and understanding of me? Well, I try.)

We've figured out that he's been away at private schools, but for some reason has come to do the last year and a half here with us in Athenwood. You might think that a shady fellow who's only been around for two days probably doesn't deserve to be on my list of Important Characters, but Helena is totally head over heels, and so I kind of have to mention him. I wouldn't be surprised if they do end up together—in addition to being passionate, that girl is as stubborn as frozen beeswax. The minute she set eyes on him she decided that he was The One, and by yesterday she'd picked names for their kids, their cats, and their peacocks, and written a whole book of poems to him. That's how she is. Devoted doesn't begin to describe it.

SO, moving on. Ooo, should I talk about me? Not that I'll have to, since my life story will no doubt be familiar to my millions of adoring fans. But I can at least record this right now: I may only be sixteen years old, but I KNOW I'm going to be a famous actress someday. That's my destiny (as Helena would say . . . except Helena would be talking about Dmitri, which is plain silliness)!

Mr. Duke hasn't caught on to my destiny yet, but what do you expect from a man who thinks an Entirely! Blue! Set! is the most innovative idea in the history of theater. Yeesh. It is kind of spectacularly unfair, though. He keeps giving Helena all the lead roles just because she's pretty. And listen, I love Helena, but I don't think standing on a balcony opining in a tragic voice is "acting." It's like she doesn't care what the character is about; she just likes the costumes and the sound of the words. She's told me herself that she thinks I'm a better actress than her (I AM), and that she doesn't even enjoy being onstage. Is she kidding? I LOVE being onstage! I like it when people pay attention to me! I am SO ready for my hordes of adoring fans!

I keep my fingers crossed every year anyway. Auditions tomorrow! Yay! I can always dream, right? I'd be such a bad-ass Juliet. I tried to convince Alex to audition for once this year, but he was like, *"Romeo and Juliet?* Are you kidding? There's not enough money on this EARTH to pay me to do something like that. I'll stick to hanging lights and hammering sets, thanks very much." Well, since that's what I'll probably be doing anyway, I suppose I should appreciate that—I mean, imagine if he got cast as Romeo opposite SOME OTHER GIRL! It would be like the end of the world, even if it was Helena, who I can at least trust not to try anything. ☺

Hmmmm. Speaking of Alex, I wonder what he's doing right now. Certainly not homework, I hope. Because while I agree with Helena that this diary thing will be a wonderful "vehicle for expression" and "repository of memories" (repository?), I don't think she was taking into account how much SUNSHINE there might be outside—in February, no less! So I think it would be perfectly justifiable for me to stop right here and head outside to try and find someone to go for a walk with me. Maybe someone with floppy brown hair, and mischievous brown eyes, and cute, sticky-out ears— AAAAAH what is HAPPENING to me! It's like Helena's nonsense is contagious! Maybe it's the diary . . . I'd better stop writing at once!

Cartwheels, pinwheels, waterwheels,
Hermia! ☺

Thursday, 20 February
Dear Diary,

It happened again today! I'm absolutely going to explode if our gym teacher doesn't stop doing this. I really can't see how anyone gets us confused.

I'm tall—she's short. I'm pale—she's tan. I'm elegant—she's bouncy. I have an air of mysterious grace and charming melancholy. She *has fits where she can't stop laughing and still wears overalls to school, even though we are juniors now, for heaven's sake, and should be setting an example of maturity and sophistication for the underclassmen.*

Ok, so she's also my best friend, but just because we spend all our time together doesn't make it logical for all these people to keep calling me Hermia! Does it? I think not. And the frustrating part is that nobody seems to call her Helena by accident. It's like there's just lots of Hermia. I don't see WHY. Maybe because Hermia is such a weird name. But Helena is unusual too, isn't it? In a striking, graceful, entirely *memorable way?*

I suppose if I were going to be anybody but myself, I'd want to be Hermia. It would be interesting to be self-confident and cheerful all the time, or at least, to seem that way . . . I know she does get sad or insecure, but only to me, and not very often. My father thinks it's funny that we're friends because I "don't seem like the type to suffer happy people gladly" (thanks, Dad), but she's not one of those annoying happy people, you know? Ok, it can be a little much sometimes. But she is my best friend in the world, seriously.

Still, when one has spent most of one's teenage years trying to cultivate an air of elegance, nobility, and aloof charm, like a queen in an ancient epic, it can be downright maddening to have people confuse you with a hyperactive people person whose catchphrase is "Enthusiasm! Here we go! Yay!" Plus, I'm me, myself, and you'd think that would be distinctive enough for people.

At least Dmitri never calls me Hermia. He appreciates my unique and subtle nature. At least, I assume so; he has yet to call me anything at all, but I caught his soulful eyes gazing in my direction more than once, let me tell you. Three times, in fact, to be specific: once before lunch, once during AP physics, and once after my deeply moving rendition of that sonnet I wrote for our Elizabethan literature elective.

Hermia laughed and said he was probably watching the clock behind me, but I should think I would know the difference between the enchanted gaze of a soul mate and the blank stare of someone who's bored. I mean really. I can tell that this young man is destined for me. Our fates are linked together like . . . like rays of moonlight pouring in silver silken silence over dappled forest glades. There, that was poetic; I shall copy it out neatly and commit it to heart so I can say it to my beloved one day and he can be duly awestruck. It's been four whole days now! I think it's about time he realized our spiritual bond, don't you?

At least auditions today went well. I know I shouldn't want to be the lead again, but I do, I have to confess. I'm not particularly fond of being onstage in front of legions of people, but I do love

*saying Shakespeare's words and wearing the
beautiful costumes and imagining that I'm a
noble Italian heroine. And Juliet is one of my
favorites—she's so rhapsodic, and untouchable,
and always says the most perfect, poetic things.
Besides, whatever Hermia says, I think it's
romantic to die for love. Romeo and Juliet
understood what soul mates are all about. They
knew that they were destined for each other,
and they would never be able to live without their
true love. It's so beautiful!*

*Even if I did have to read with Nick, who
kept stammering and blushing and couldn't even
look at me the whole time. I don't know why; I
was perfectly friendly and not in the least bit
stuck-up. It's so strange that he even decided to
audition in the first place! I suppose Theo's sign
worked; there were quite a lot of football players
there. VERY bizarre.*

*Yours by moonlight,
Helena*

My Deeply Moving Sonnet
by Helena Naples

In all the world there shall be only him
For me, and I his one true love shall be.
We'll find our fate through shadows dark and dim
And thenceforth live in perfect harmony.

Until that moment I shall be alone.
Until he comes to lift my soul aloft,
I've turned away the young men I have known,
I wait for eyes of brown I've dreamed of oft.

O me! Wherefore must I so long await
The blissful day when our two souls will twine.
I know I must be patient, trust in fate.
But I stand prepared to say my heart is thine.

Soul mate, find me soon, I do entreat thee,
Capture my heart and let us love completely.

Date: Thursday 20 February 22:13:00
From: AmazonGrrrl! [HermiaJ@athenwood.edu]
To: Poetess [HelenaN@athenwood.edu]
Subject: Dreamboats in Tights!

Helena!

GUESS WHO showed up to audition right at the end this afternoon? It was after you'd gone home, and there were only a couple of people still reading, and Mr. Duke was getting ready to close up, and Polly and I were talking about the lighting plot and if she'd need to rent any lights for the show, when in walks:

DMITRI!

Yes, your one and only!

He strolled in all la-di-da and is like, hey, I want to audition. Of course Mr. Duke is just THRILLED to bits because OH MY GOD IT'S A BOY! IN THE THEATER! (he had the same over-the-top reaction to every single football player, too—and is it me, or were there an awful lot of them there?). So he's like, absolutely, here you go, and drags me onto the stage to read with Dmitri (is that a good sign for my chances of being cast? I can't tell!).

Let me tell you, darling, that boy really looooooooooooooooooooves himself. Not that there's anything wrong with that! But it was kind of funny. He hardly seemed to notice I was there; he kept strutting back and forth and proclaiming to the aisles, like

Juliet was actually hanging out in the back of the theater instead of right there on stage next to him, hello! I had a really hard time not laughing. But apart from ignoring me completely, he seemed to be a pretty good actor, so maybe he'll get cast! And it can be your romantic dream come true—because I mean, seriously, like there's any chance Mr. Duke isn't going to cast you as Juliet. He had you read about a million times.

I'll be lucky if I get to be the Nurse, but I wouldn't be at all surprised to find myself cast as "The Vine on Juliet's Balcony That Dmitri Steps on to Get Up to Where He Can Declare His Undying Love to Our Heroine." Woo! One day, Helena, just you wait. One day I will get to audition for real theater people, and they will discover me, and I will be off to fame and fortune and most importantly, fame. ☺

Hermia!

P.S. One of the disadvantages of staying late at the theater is you run the risk of witnessing the most shocking things. I was sweeping the stage for Polly, right there, in plain view! when Mr. Duke comes up to her and is like: "Polly, darling, this has been the most exquisite day! Let us celebrate with wine and dinner!" and she was like: "Theo, I've told you before. No, never, and absolutely not. And in case that wasn't perfectly clear: over my dead body."

But he goes on—just as if there ISN'T an innocent student mere FEET away who could be PERMANENTLY TRAUMATIZED by outrageous things like old people asking each other out (EW!)—"But Polly, my love, it doesn't have to be a date! You could give me your expert opinion on the auditions we saw today!" And she goes: "Oh, I can tell you what I think in about ten seconds flat. No need to waste an entire perfectly good evening on *that*." And then he followed her off behind a curtain and I didn't hear the rest of it. I wonder what she does think? Not that he would listen to her anyway, but I'd certainly be curious . . .

Friday, February 21

Dear Future Me!

I've got it! I've got the perfect mid-conversation beginning for my Best-selling Life Story! It's got everything—humor, drama, pathos (ok, I don't know what that is), unspoken love, mystery, jelly beans . . .

It all started at lunch today.

"I can't believe you're going to miss my party," Helena said (for like the millionth time).

"I'm *sorry*," I said. "You know my mom gets me for spring break, and she wants to take me on some sort of retreat. And you know I wish I was going to be here for your birthday, but what can I do?"

She pretended to look thoughtful for a minute, then said: "I *suppose* you could try bringing me back a particularly exotic and thrilling present."

"From Vermont? You might be that lucky," I teased. "Besides, it's going to be a totally intimidating party anyway. I'm surprised your dad even let you invite me, along with all the dignitaries and official-type people that will be attending."

"Yes, it does seem sometimes like this party is more for him than me," she mused. "But it could be fascinating—when else do we get to dress up in elegant gowns and practice the ballroom dancing they taught us in sixth grade?"

"Eeeek." I shuddered. "We are SO lucky I'm not going to be there."

"Don't look now," Alex said, sliding his tray onto the table and scooting onto the bench next to me. "But a certain someone is totally checking you out, Helena." He nodded at her and gave me his cute, lopsided smile. (MELT! If I were prone to swooning, this would be one of those moments. So it's lucky I'm not, because, seriously, in the high school cafeteria?)

Helena's eyes lit up. "Is it Dmitri?" she whispered urgently.

"Dmitri?"

"Helena's picked out a soul mate at last," I informed him. "The oh-so-poetic-looking new guy? Not that we've scouted out his whole schedule yet or anything, but I *believe* he has PE with you third period." I winked at Helena, who did an admirable job of not looking too mortified.

"No way." Alex gave up wrestling with his milk carton and handed it to me. "Dmitri? Seriously? You like *that* guy, Helena?" I pried open the side he hadn't completely destroyed and handed it back to him.

"What?" she said, turning pink. "He seems . . . deep."

"He's a jerk. Trust me—I know him."

"RRREALLY?" I said, immensely curious. "How? Why? Tell us absolutely everything this minute."

"It's a long, fairly embarrassing story," he said. (See? I told you there was mystery!) "Let's just say he's not your type at all, Helena."

"Oh? And what exactly do you know about *my* type, Alexander Sanders?" she said archly.

I came very close to snorting milk up my nose when she said that. I can't help it! I think Alex's full name is hilarious! I mean, what were his parents thinking? Alex Sanders? WERE they thinking? It's so much fun to say, though. Except Alex isn't quite as amused by it as I am, for some reason.

"Uh-oh," I said, trying to keep it light. "She's doing the full name thing! Time to back away slowly, hands where we can see 'em. Also, she has a point. Speaking as the best friend, even *I'm* not sure what her type is, although I have a hunch Johnny Depp might fit the bill."

"Whatever," Alex joked, mocking me. "He's, like, totally old and stuff."

"I'm serious, Alexander," Helena interrupted. "What do you think my type is, and what precisely disqualifies Dmitri already?"

"Whereas what *I* want to know," I said, "is who *was* checking Helena out, if not Dmitri."

"Oh, right!" Alex said. "I'll give you a hint: two words. The first one is half of a half, and the second one is the opposite of front."

"What?" said Helena.

"Hey, I thought quarterback was one word," I said.

"WHAT?" said Helena.

"A gold star for the little lady," Alex pronounced,

then backtracked rapidly. "That is to say, the lady who is only little relative to other, much taller ladies, although, of course, clearly the perfect height for her own, most-perfect-in-every-way self."

Helena gave me one of her *riiiight, he's not madly in love with you at ALL* looks and said: "Are you talking about Nick Weaver?"

"Ding ding ding! He's cute, right? Like, way cuter than Dmitri?" Alex said hopefully, although none too wisely.

"Please!" Helena rolled her eyes. "Young ladies of my poetic disposition do not date football jocks, ok? Besides, Nick totally hates me, and in any case, it is eminently clear to everyone at this table who isn't you that Dmitri is in every way ideally suited for me, and I for him."

Alex raised his eyebrows at me and I shrugged. I was still trying to think of a clever way to respond to the perfect-in-every-way remark, preferably a way that would convey that I think he's perfect, too, and hey, maybe we should date!

"That's what everyone thinks, huh?" he said.

I sensed the moment might have passed.

"I thought all girls wanted to date football players," Alex said, stabbing his "meat loaf." "Isn't that right, Hermia? I mean, *you* did."

Urp. Helena sprang to my defense.

"Mistakes like Peter Quincey are inevitable in the perilous terrain of adolescent dating, Alexander."

"Yeah, and I was like, *way* younger and stupider back then," I said. "I think my tastes have *clearly* matured in the last six months. I'm ready to date *much better* guys now." See, wasn't that a hint? A really obvious hint? How is he not picking up on these?

"Huh," he said. "So, you ready for that history test?"

Helena rolled her eyes at me (see, SHE gets my hints!) and stood up.

"That's my cue to exit stage left," she said. "You guys study; I'm going to stop by the theater and see if by some miraculous chance Theo has posted the cast list yet. I'll see you in gym, ok, Hermia?"

"Sure," I said, "but remember, if the cast list is up, you can tell me it's there, but you can't tell me what it says."

"Still?" she protested. "What if it's positively thrilling?"

"Hey, every great actress has to have her superstitions. Mine is that I need to see the cast list myself, on my own. It's for good luck."

"Ok, fine," she said. "But if it doesn't work for the third year in a row, I think you should develop a new superstition for next year." Ouch! I mean really. Alex gave me a sympathetic glance as Helena gathered her things. Look at him being all perceptive and understanding! Isn't that cute? Now if he'd only perceive the fact that we should date, everything would be perfect.

Off Helena went. As soon as the cafeteria doors closed behind her, I turned to Alex and said: "Ok, doofus. How long have you known Helena now? Two years? Have we really not picked up on the fact that it's a Bad Idea to criticize her aesthetic choices?"

"You mean Dmitri?" he said, astonished. "I didn't realize that warning her off a bad boyfriend was on the same level as telling her that *Gladiator* isn't really that great a movie." He paused, thinking. "Although, now you mention it, I can see what you mean."

"The trick is to act noncommittal," I said. "Like: oh really? You want to rent *that* movie? Huh. Yeah, that could be ok . . . or there's always *Shakespeare in Love*, of course . . . But if you say, ew, no WAY, not THAT movie, then you're totally screwed, because either you'll end up having to rent it, or she'll be silently offended for the rest of the night."

"And you think this is kind of the same?"

"Yup," I said.

"Whoops."

"Tell me about it. Now they're *definitely* going to date. Way to go, Cupid." I dug my bag of jelly beans out of my backpack and started sorting the Juicy Pears and Popcorn ones onto his tray. I mean, popcorn? Really? He's the only person I've ever met who actually likes them, which, quite frankly, is very convenient, because I go through truckloads of these things.

"What does she have against Nick Weaver, anyway?" he asked.

"She doesn't have anything against him, precisely," I explained. "We used to be friends with him, but then he asked her out, and it was a big mess, because you know Helena's theories on dating, and he hasn't really spoken to her much since then, so she's pretty sure he hates her."

"Huh," he said.

"Yeah, it's too bad, because they were friends"— *say it! be brave!*—"and you know, personally, I think it's totally possible for friends to date and still stay friends." I couldn't believe it! I couldn't believe I actually said that to him! I might as well have dropped an anvil on his head, don't you think? An anvil labeled: I LIKE YOU! DATE ME! SMOOCH ME NOW!

"Huh," he said. There was a pause as he nudged around some of the jelly beans.

"Huh?" I finally said, hopefully.

"I don't think this is Popcorn," he said, handing a jelly bean back to me. "It looks suspiciously like Toasted Marshmallow."

Dadblastfnarringschnortlegrrrrrrrr . . .

"Oops," I said, keeping it casual. "My sinister quest to hook you on other jelly bean flavors continues." He grinned at me. "So." I sighed. "Manifest Destiny, huh?"

And there you have it. All my relationships, summed up in one oh-so-significant scene. Maybe one day they'll turn it into a play. Or a movie! I think I'd be an excellent heroine, don't you? Heroically forging her shining theatrical career while winning her hero, despite all the silly obstacles along the way.

There I go again, sounding like Helena. This diary-writing stuff is dangerous!

Sunshine and stardom!
Hermia!!!

Hi Helena!
Regarding Alex—one word: OBLIVIOUS!
Oblivious!

Oblivious!

Arrrrrrrgh!

Hermia!

P.S. Have you introduced yourself to new-boy yet? You should so invite him to your party! He looks like the type who might actually know how to ballroom dance. Don't they teach that kind of thing at private schools? WEIRD.

Date: Saturday 22 February 13:02:00
From: Poetess [HelenaN@athenwood.edu]
To: AmazonGrrrl! [HermiaJ@athenwood.edu]
Subject: Saints above

HERMIA.

Is this true?

You're grounded AGAIN?

For the WHOLE weekend?!

And have I mentioned lately that your dad scares me? All I did was say: "Oh, hello, Mr. Jackson. May I please speak to Hermia?" and he sort of flipped out.

"NO, you may NOT, young lady, as she is GROUNDED until further notice, and shall remain so until she learns to speak to her father with some respect!" Then he mumbled something about you attacking him with toast? Maybe? And he practically slammed the phone down.

What in heaven's name did you do now? Haven't we talked about ways to avoid turning your dad into Mr. Tyrannical Grouch Man? Deep calming breaths, remember? Reasonable, civilized tones. It works with *my* father; I mean, yes, I rarely see him, so it's easier to avoid arguments. But seriously, Hermia. Now what am I supposed to do? Hang out with myself all weekend?

Alas, I am so forsaken.

Well, I hope you're not really in too much trouble . . . is there anything I can do to help?

lots of très supportive hugs
Helena

Date: Saturday 22 February 15:29:00
From: AmazonGrrrl! [HermiaJ@athenwood.edu]
To: Poetess [HelenaN@athenwood.edu]
Subject: ARRRRRRRRRRRR

OH my God it is SO not my fault! I am so reasonable! I'm the most reasonable, civilized person ever! He doesn't LISTEN to me! I swear!

I mean, look, he was already grumpy last night, when Alex came over for dinner. He did that thing he always does where he acts like he's never met Alex before. You know? I can't tell if he's serious or not. He really seems to think Alex is just the latest in a string of boys I've been dating, although Alex is the only one I've been bringing to dinner for like months now (oh, yeah, and we're not actually dating) (*sigh*).

It's like Dad paid attention long enough in early high school to notice that I was bringing home a different boy every month, so he stopped actually trying to tell the difference between them. And so, even though I've been friends with Alex for *well over two years* now, Dad still has the *exact same conversation* with him every time he comes for dinner: "So, what's *your* name, young man? Oh yes? And what are you studying? Ah, fine. And what sort of *career* are you looking for with a course of study like that? Yes, yes, quite right. And your opinion on our strategy in China?" It's totally funny, because you can tell Dad's not really listening. Last night Alex told him that his name was Narcissus, that he was studying self-reflection, and that he was hoping to become a flower. Dad went "Hrmmm, yes yes, what on earth is in this soup . . ." I nearly died trying *not* to die laughing.

Anyway, I came downstairs for breakfast this morning and his bad mood was even worse. Grump grump, I've been up since seven, kids today have no concept of work, always sleeping until noon, grump grump. (Plus, by the way, it was totally not noon. It was like, eleven-fifteen, or something! What does he want from me?)

So I TRIED to be all cheerful and I started talking about the auditions, because I thought they went really well and I was excited, right? I don't know what I said—yap yap acting is fun—but he started looking all dark and glowering, the way he does sometimes. And THEN the phone rang. WELL. Of

COURSE it was Mom, which didn't help Dad's mood at all. But he gave me the phone and I started telling Mom about the auditions.

I guess I forgot Dad was in the room, because I said: "Oooh, hey Mom, do you think Olivia could give me some advice about auditioning sometime? I mean, she's a successful actress, right?"

Mom said, "Sure, honey. She'll probably be joining us for part of the retreat over your spring break, so you can talk to her about it then."

I said, "How did she get started anyway? Do you know?"

And she said: "She did a few summer internships in college. When she gets back from grocery shopping, do you want me to have her call you?"

"No, no," I said, already picturing Dad answering the phone and finding HER on the other end. "I'll talk to her at the retreat. But a summer internship sounds awesome."

Doesn't this all sound perfectly innocent? And reasonable? And moreover private, so one might think that certain grown-ups in the room might be minding their own business instead of snooping for things to get mad about? YES INDEED.

Well, so I get off the phone, and Dad immediately starts in on me. "Don't you start getting ideas in that head of yours, young lady," that kind of thing. "I don't want to hear any more about you trying to be an actress. It's an unstable, unprofitable career fit only for slacker layabouts and no-good wife-stealers, yada yada yada." (Maybe not in those words, but the underlying point is ALL TOO CLEAR.) "It's a good thing my friend Mr. Duke is far too sensible to encourage your delusions of grandeur by casting you," and so on.

What was I supposed to do? NOT get mad? He's questioning my whole future here! So then there was the yelling and the screaming and ok, possibly some toast-throwing, although I didn't MEAN to do that, I just picked up my plate in a dramatic, expressive way and the toast kind of launched itself . . . Anyway, that's not really the point. The point is I was grounded by eleven-thirty, my dad is a chowderhead, and now I'm stuck in my room all weekend. Even the "I have to go study with Helena" thing didn't work. Can you believe it? Life is SO unfair.

I'm going to go surf the Internet for summer internships. THAT'LL teach him, mwa ha-ha.

As for what you should do, I gave you your assignment yesterday, remember? WELL? Have you invited what's-his-face to your party? Has he talked to you yet at all? Remember: I said by the end of the weekend, or I'll go tell him myself to ask you out, and that's SO eighth grade.

Good luck! E-mail me later, ok? I'm in desperate need of signs that there is still sane life in the universe out there . . .

Hermia!

P.S. I forgot to tell you—Polly said she thinks Mr. Duke probably won't post the cast list until Tuesday. TUESDAY! ARGH! The agony!

Date: Saturday 22 February 20:45:00
From: Poetess [HelenaN@athenwood.edu]
To: AmazonGrrrl! [HermiaJ@athenwood.edu]
Subject: Ah. Clarity Ensues.

Ok, that does make sense. Your dad is really the height of injustice, isn't he? It's like he's impervious to reason. I can see how you become inextricably entangled in these quarrels with him.

What's-his-face indeed, Hermia! That is no way to speak of my truly beloved future husband and soul mate. Try to think of him as a sort of brother-in-law. I don't want our children to lose respect for their father from overhearing any of your ABSURD comments.

And as a matter of fact, I *did* talk to him today! I remember every word he said. I have impressed them all deep into my heart. And I am quite certain that he felt the same way and, despite your rude remarks, I think if you saw the way he smiled at me that you would have to agree. And I think you would also have to be extremely impressed at my ability to preserve a dignified demeanor, despite all the insalubrious circumstances aligned against me.

But I was cool and graceful nonetheless. Even our initial encounter, when I dropped all my books on his feet and crashed sidelong into a spiral staircase, was clearly a carefully engineered maneuver to impress upon him his *own* clumsiness and great good fortune to have knocked over such a charming damsel.

You may recollect (although I suspect you do NOT) that we have an art history presentation due this Thursday on two great artists of the last fifty years, and so, surmising that you might have little opportunity for gathering research while trapped in your room by your father, I nobly took it upon myself to spend Saturday in the library, by myself, studiously taking notes for the both of us.

Imagine my surprise to discover that none other than Dmitri himself actually has a part-time job in the reference section on the weekends. WELL! (Ok, perhaps he mentioned this when he introduced himself in physics class, but one could hardly expect me to remember such details about anyone's everyday life, now could one?)

So of course I pretended not to notice him at first. I glided nonchalantly through the shelves, selecting various books with a bright, contemplative expression. This, however, had no apparent effect, as he continued in his clever charade of sitting on a stool reading, oblivious of the outside world. Ha! Well, two could play that little game. I took my books over to a table that was in his range of sight, although not too close, and I sat with my better profile toward him and applied myself to my studies, allowing my hair occasionally to drape gracefully over the page.

Out of the corner of my eye he did appear to be virtually motionless, but I am sure that if I could have examined him more carefully I would have observed him glancing up at me periodically in timid fascination. However, the dear boy must be terribly shy, because he still refrained from approaching me, even though I am so clearly his soul mate.

At long (VERY long) length, he suddenly closed his book with a snap and, gathering a pile of books from a nearby table, set off down one of the aisles. By this point I had filled sheets and sheets of paper with my elegant handwriting to illustrate my academic nature, and you had better not complain that my notes have surprisingly little to do with the Guerilla Girls and perchance too much to do with potential wedding plans, little Miss I'm-grounded-how-can-I-possibly-study.

Seeing him disappear amidst the shelves, it occurred to me that the books I had were not sufficiently informative, so I swept them all up and proceeded into the stacks at once to find new ones. As I drifted gently along, I could hear him on the other side of the shelves, sliding books into place firmly, quietly humming to himself. (He's musical, too! Such perfection in one mortal being!)

As I picked three more books off the shelf, I could hear him moving away from me down the shelves, so I started moving slightly more rapidly toward the end—figuring he'd move to the next aisle, and I'd move into his, you see. But suddenly I couldn't hear where he was, so I sashayed quickly around the corner and crashed rather suddenly right into him, dropping all my books on his feet and bouncing off a nearby staircase before landing in a (very elegant) heap on the floor.

"Whoa. Are you all right?" he said. *Are you all right?*—the first words he ever spoke to me! Isn't that sweet? And caring? And heroic? You see, he's not as bad as you think.

I debated swooning, but I wasn't sure I could do it convincingly enough. So I tossed my hair back, gazed up at him beguilingly, and said, in my most enchanting tone, "I am now, stranger."

Ok, then I'll admit he looked a little confused. Perhaps he hadn't felt the spark of soul mate recognition yet. It's perfectly understandable. I've heard that sometimes it takes longer for boys to catch on. They're a little thick that way, even the perfect ones. So I added quickly, "I mean, silly me, making such a mess. I assure you I've never dropped this many books before in my life."

And then he smiled! He *smiled!* And said: "Oh, I have. Plenty of times. It's a skill you sort of pick up with the job."

And THEN do you KNOW what he DID? Can you even IMAGINE? He reached out and *****took my hand!!!!!******* I would have fainted right there and then, except he hauled me to my feet so fast I could barely even stand gracefully, and at that point I figured falling right back over, even in a very delicate manner, might not exactly have impressed him with my cleverness. Then he put down the two books he was holding and started helping me gather mine together.

I tried the tinkling laugh I've been practicing all week, and said: "Wait, now I remember; I do know you. Aren't you in a few of my classes at school?"

I was about to apologize for not remembering his name, when he said: "Oh, yeah, that's right. I'm sorry, I don't remember your name," which I thought was an absolutely *brilliant* tactical move, even if it left me somewhat taken aback. (Now, I know what you're thinking, silly Hermia, and it's ridiculous; of course he really did remember my name. He merely had to act like he didn't, in case I turned out to be one of those snobbish girls—which I so am not, ahem, Mr. Nick—that look down on boys who actually try to talk to them, although how he could mistake me for one of them I'll never know, since I don't *think* he's connected me to my dad yet.)

SO, I had to adopt the opposite tactic, naturally, to make my dazzling memory and lack of snobbishness perfectly clear.

"That's all right—it's Helena. Isn't your name . . . Dmitri? The one who's been away at boarding school all my life? I mean, all your life?" Whoops. He didn't seem to notice, though.

"Yeah, that's right. Dad thought I ought to come back here for the last couple of years, though, to spend some time at home before college and meet some Athenwood people." Then he said something about how many important upper-class types live in this town, but I didn't really hear him, because I was thinking: Meet some Athenwood people! That's *me*! He was guided by FATE to cross paths with me, so that our souls could be drawn together! I was nearly overwhelmed by the presence of destiny making itself so strongly felt, but then he picked up his books and started to move away.

"Well! How do you like Athenwood?!" I chirped brightly, while maintaining as much nonchalance as possible.

"It's fine. That theater director seems cool."

"Theo? He's terrific," I said. "Did you try out for the play?" (Look at me, being all suave and non-stalkery!)

"Yeah. I acted a lot at my last school, so I have kind of an unfair advantage, but it would be great to play Romeo, so I figured I'd go for it. Anyway, I have to get back to work. See you Monday," Dmitri said, and turned to go.

See you Monday! Monday! He practically said "I'll look forward to seeing you Monday." I mean, the subtext was definitely there. I decided it was time for a decisive strike. After all, we've already lost almost a whole WEEK in this not-talking, still-have-to-meet-each-other phase—how much of our lives did he really want to miss puttering around with schoolbooks when we could begin immediately going about being in love and spending every waking moment together? I didn't want to have to wait until I was *twenty* or something.

"Oh, Dmitri," I said, with astonishing calm, "by the way, my father's having a sort of birthday party ball-type thing for me in a few weeks, to start off our spring holiday. Would you be interested in coming? It's sort of a fancy affair, and there should be a number of important Athenwood people there, if you're interested in meeting them."

And *do you know* what Dmitri said?

He said: "Sure."

Sure!

This is definitely true love.

I got my coat, produced the invitation I've been smuggling about in there for just such an occasion as this, smiled my dazzling smile, and sashayed gracefully out the door, completely forgetting my notebook and school bag. I had to pay my stupid little brother to go in and get them for me.

But still! Dmitri is coming to my house! Very soon! For a ball! What am I going to wear? It is beyond tragic that you aren't going to be here, Hermia. Who is going to fix my hair? Dad? My brother the brat?

If only Mother were still alive, although I have no idea if she would have been good at fixing hair anyhow—I imagine so; you must remember how elegant she was when we were little, when you came to stay with us after your mother left. In the pictures Mother always looks graceful and perfect—that's what I'm going to look like eventually! Hopefully by my birthday!

You'll have to help me choose a dress. I can't believe you're going to be gone for the whole two weeks of spring break. It's going to be *so* boring without you. Well, unless I manage to occupy myself by spending time with Dmitri, of course. Tra la la . . .

See, Hermia, I did talk to him, so there. Sometimes I can be just as brave as you.

To fan the moonbeams from his sleeping eyes,

Helena

ACT II

March & April

FELLOW THESPIANS!

Thrilling news about this year's
Athenwood High School Spring Production!

We've decided to try something different*!*

We've decided to try something daring*!*

*We've decided to try something
truly* Shakespearean*:*

AN ALL-MALE CAST!

Just like they did in the Elizabethan era!

It's going to be FANTASTIC!

Thanks to everyone for trying out! And now, without
further ado, here is the *Romeo and Juliet* cast list:

Romeo Montague	Nick Weaver
Juliet Capulet	Frank Flutie
Tybalt	Peter Quincey
Mercutio	Dmitri Gilbert
Nurse	Rob Taylor
Friar Lawrence	Tom O'Kinter
Paris	Leo Sung

Remaining Parts TBA

* Technical assistants still required; please contact
Ms. Mason in the art department if interested.

I stared at the board in shock. I had arisen practically at the crack of dawn Tuesday morning specifically to get to school early and see the cast list right away. And THIS was it?

What was Hermia going to say?

This was unbelievable. Theo had done some appalling things before—like, I'll admit, casting me as Blanche DuBois when I was just a freshman and there were plenty of senior girls above me who really deserved it—but this was going entirely too far.

Casting only boys—and mostly football players at that! When there were dozens of talented girls in this school that he consistently ignored. Not the least of whom was my own best friend.

Hermia was going to be devastated. She wouldn't let on, because that's not what she does, but inside she'd be horribly hurt. After all, she's been so loyal to this theater program—no matter how small her part, she always shows up, always pitches in, always spends practically as much time on the set as our technical director, Polly Mason, does. And she is *such* an amazing actress; it's simply absurd how Theo has managed to miss it for three years. I'll be the first to admit that she's more talented than I am, plus theater is what she wants to *do* with her life.

To be honest, I was rather hurt for myself as well. Hadn't I been a good lead in the last few plays? Didn't Theo like me anymore? Did he really think a football player named *Frank* would be a better, more soulful Juliet than I would? And didn't he *realize* what a perfect Romeo and Juliet Dmitri and I would have been?

I realized that I was dangerously close to crying just as I

heard voices coming into the theater lobby—big burly male voices. I did *not* want to see any of them. There wasn't time to escape gracefully out the back, so I ducked quickly behind a curtain and hid.

Just as I suspected: Nick Weaver and his macho buddies. They were joking as they swaggered in.

"NICK," one of them roared as they came through the door. It sounded like Pete, Hermia's incredibly sleazy ex. "I can't believe this plan of yours, man! You better have been cast, is all I can say. This is the lamest way to get a g—"

"Shut *up*," Nick interrupted, and there were brief scuffling sounds. As far as I've been able to ascertain from across the cafeteria, these guys mostly interact by wrestling and pummeling each other. After about a minute of that, Nick continued: "Come on, I know it's a long shot, but I figure I could do, like, Gregory, or the Apothecary or something, you know?"

I was a little impressed at that. Nick Weaver could name minor characters in a Shakespeare play? Will wonders never cease. Maybe he had read it, after all. Still, I had a feeling these boys were in for a serious shock.

"Dude," one of the others, maybe Tom, said, in a hushed voice.

"WHOA," said another, possibly Leo, whom I have never heard say anything other than "dude" and "whoa." I took a certain wicked glee in picturing how he would deal with "Immoderately she weeps for Tybalt's death" or "These times of woe afford no time to woo." (Although, come to think of it, that last one did at least feature one of the two words in his vocabulary.)

"What?" said Pete.

"Check this out," said Tom.

There was a pause as Pete and presumably Nick finally read the sign. I continued to reflect bitterly on the vagaries of fate and our theater director.

"Whoa," Leo said again.

"Gentlemen, we are *screwed*," said Tom.

"What the—I'm a *nurse?*" said a fifth voice, evidently Rob. (Not the Rob that Hermia dated, though; that one graduated last year, and would never be seen within a mile of a football field).

"Oh my God," said Nick.

"Nick . . . ," Pete said darkly. "Tell me this is a joke."

"Uh—," said Nick. The theater door banged open.

"Hey, guys! What's up? How's it hanging?" Ah. Frank had arrived. I stifled a giggle. Frank Flutie was a sophomore, one of the shortest guys in the high school. His dad was someone important, so they let him be an alternate for the football team, although there wasn't a chance in the world that they'd ever let him play. Still, he followed the jocks around and they seemed to tolerate him fine, mainly because Nick was nice to him, and for the most part the other guys followed Nick's lead in everything.

"Got a surprise for you, Frank," Pete said, still in that low, halfway-to-furious voice.

"Did I get cast? Seriously? No way! Did I?"

"Oh, you got a biiiiiiiiiiiiiiiiiig part, my man," said Pete.

"Really? Am I Romeo? You know, I thought I'd be a great Romeo. He is only like fifteen in the play, you know. Did I get Romeo?"

"Not . . . exactly," said Tom.

"Take a look," Pete said expansively.

Another brief silence. I could picture the look Frank was

giving Nick—sort of a *Is this for real?* and *What's the cool way to react here?* and *Help!!!* all rolled into one.

"Gaaaaack," was the strangled response he managed to muster.

"You're going to be the prettiest Juliet this school has ever seen," Rob snorted.

"Unless she's overshadowed by her mighty fine nurse, of course," Tom said.

More sounds of scuffling. Over them I could hear Nick's voice.

"I can't believe this. I really can't. I don't know what's going on, guys, but this has to be a mistake."

"Yeguurk," Frank retorted helpfully.

"You called this play, man," Pete said.

"Yeah, but Mr. Duke is, like, the coach—he gets to pick the players," Nick said. "I just can't believe he wouldn't cast Helena as Juliet," he added, so quietly I barely caught what he said. But I'm sure that was it: Helena as Juliet. Which was really kind of sweet. I couldn't help feeling flattered, and a little charmed. Plus, of course, I completely felt the same way.

"Maybe we should go talk to Mr. Duke," Nick suggested. "He can't be serious about this."

"Dude," Leo agreed.

"Hurmagah," Frank squeaked.

There were some grunts and a few smacking sounds as Nick separated the others, and then our glorious spring production cast bundled themselves out the door and off down the hall. I could hear Leo yelling "DUDE!" as the door slammed shut behind them.

I slid down the wall until I was sitting on the ground, still hidden by the velvet curtain. How was Hermia going to react? At least we could commiserate with each other on this one ... Surely that would be an improvement over the times when I got the lead and she didn't, perhaps?

But a sinking feeling in my chest was warning me: she was going to be utterly destroyed.

> **Helena!**
> **I still haven't been able to stop laughing. Miz Harpy is giving me VERY severe looks and Alex keeps glancing at me like I'm crazy. But SERIOUSLY!**
> **An all-male cast for *Romeo and Juliet*?**
> **The utterly brainless Pete Quincey forced to memorize Shakespeare?**
> **FRANK FLUTIE as Juliet?**
> ***hee hee hee hee hee hee hee hee hee hee hee hee hee hee hee hee hee hee hee!***
> **Ok, I'm going to try concentrating *really hard* on the implications of Western expansion, and see if that can stop me from giggling all over the B I got on that last exam. Stupid history! Like we need it! When there's LEO SUNG ACTING in our future!**
> **Hermia!**

Poetess: Hermia? Are you actually on, or did you forget to turn off your computer?

AmazonGrrrl!: No, I'm here! I'm stuck in my room because Dad couldn't find me after school again today. And then he didn't react very well when I tried to give him a tutorial on the voice-mail system. ☺

Poetess: I couldn't find you after school, either. Where did you disappear to?

AmazonGrrrl!: Sorry about that . . . I had a feeling if I went into the theater and actually saw Mr. Duke, I'd have some sort of hysterical laughing fit, which would have been very unprofessional. ☺ So Alex and I went to the library, and then we just walked around for a while. Have I mentioned lately how much I like him? ☺

Poetess: Only a couple of times. ;) So, are you ok? Really ok?

AmazonGrrrl!: Sure, of course! You mean about the cast list? I think it's funny, don't you? ☺

Poetess: Well, sure . . . it is . . . and I believe you think so . . . but I know you, Hermia. Yes, you normally use lots of smiley faces, but when you have one for almost every sentence, it generally means you're covering for something.

AmazonGrrrl!: Really? I do that?

Poetess: You do, actually.

Poetess: Hermia? You still there?

AmazonGrrrl!: Man, I need to get me some less perceptive friends. Alex kept asking me what was wrong, too.

Poetess: So you are upset?

AmazonGrrrl!: No, I'm not upset—I mean, how can you be upset at something that crazy? It would be like getting mad at my dog for chewing holes in all my dad's socks. I know, in the grand scheme of things, that it's wrong and totally unfair to the socks, but it's also *really funny*, plus you know she doesn't know any better. The same way Mr. Duke thinks he's doing something very clever and innovative, when he's really being kind of a big dumbass.

AmazonGrrrl!: The point is, what I realized, especially while I was talking with Alex, is that I need to stop hoping Mr. Duke will come to his senses about my acting. I need to go out and make my own fame and fortune; that's what real actors have to do, right? So if I want to be a superstar one day, I'd better start working on it now, and I can't count on our misogynist high school theater director helping me to do that.

AmazonGrrrl!: ☺ See, nothing to worry about! ☺ It's just made me more determined, that's all.

Poetess: Oh. Wow. Really? Ok . . . that's great.

AmazonGrrrl!: At least my dad is psyched. He loves it when I don't get cast. I think he pretty much wishes every play in the world was all male, so I couldn't be in any of them.

Poetess: He simply has no appreciation of your genius, that's all.

AmazonGrrrl!: Any new Dmitri news?

Poetess: Ooo, yes! I saw him briefly after school in the theater, checking the list. He looked a shade more melancholy than usual . . . like a heavy weight was pressing against his soul . . .

AmazonGrrrl!: So, none too pleased, then?

Poetess: I wished I could sweep his golden hair off his manly brow and comfort him with my presence, but since he doesn't really know me that well yet, I had to content myself with imagining the day when our entwined hearts will instantly draw us to each other in moments of woe and cosmic upheaval, such as this.

AmazonGrrrl!: Riiiight. What's he so woeful about, anyway? He got Mercutio! Maybe he's offended that they didn't cast him as Romeo. Maybe he wishes *he* was getting to sweep Frank Flutie off "her" feet. *hee hee hee*

Poetess: Or PERHAPS he has the noble and sensitive soul one would expect from my destined truly beloved, and he is deeply wounded at the injustice done to our entire gender.

AmazonGrrrl!: Er. Yeah. I bet that's it. ;)

Poetess: I kind of feel sorry for Nick, though.

AmazonGrrrl!: Nick? Nick WEAVER? The one who "hates" you?

Poetess: Well, yes, not THAT sorry for him. But he did look very sheepish all day, didn't you notice? Like this was somehow his fault. Don't you remember how he used to take the blame for everything? Like in fourth grade, when we thoroughly drowned his mother's entire flower garden by playing in the sprinklers?

AmazonGrrrl!: Hey, yeah—I do remember! That was YOUR idea! But he told his mom it was his, so she got all mad at him and took his trucks away, or something.

Poetess: His football, actually. For a week! I did feel rather remorseful about that.

AmazonGrrrl!: But you gave him cookies to make up for it. No wonder he liked you. I should try that cookie trick on Alex . . .

Poetess: Anyway, Nick had that same expression today. But I couldn't bring myself to speak to him—after all, convincing all his macho friends to try out WAS his idea, heaven only knows why.

AmazonGrrrl!: I heard that Mr. Duke is going to try and get them extra credit for their English classes, too, in addition to the elective thing, just to make sure they don't drop out. Isn't that unfair? He never had to bribe US to stay in plays!

Poetess: Does this mean that you're not going to work on the play at all?

AmazonGrrrl!: No, I'll probably still help Polly with the sets and lighting, but I think I'm going to start really seriously looking for some sort of summer theater internship now. Are you going to work on the play?

AmazonGrrrl!: Wait, silly question. Dmitri's in it, after all, isn't he? ;)

Poetess: Quite so! And he'll be needing a costume, one might imagine.

AmazonGrrrl!: So he'll be needing someone to *measure* him for the costume . . . someone to help him with the quick changes . . .

Poetess: Hermia! Stop that! You shocking wicked creature!

AmazonGrrrl!: Who, me? *innocent expression*

Poetess: Those inspired by the spirit of true love have no need for such transparent machinations to bring them together.

AmazonGrrrl!: Still, he will at some point have to take his shirt off in front of you, right?

Poetess: One might imagine. ;)

Wednesday, March 12
Dear Diary,
 Today was so odd, I almost don't know how
to describe it. I waver between delight and dismay
and end up finding myself altogether embroiled
in confusion. I know the course of true love never
did run smooth, but when soul mates are involved,
I would have imagined one might bypass all the

misunderstandings and bewilderment that seem to characterize most of the romantic entanglements I have witnessed. (Although, to be fair, since most of those featured wonderful Hermia and a host of dreadful guys, perhaps I might not have the widest range of experience to draw from at this point.)

In any case, I should set down the events of today, so that I may peruse them at my leisure in future, happier times, when Dmitri and I are joyfully together and can laugh at all the silly obstacles that once seemed determined to come between us.

Spring break starts next week, and it turns out Ms. Mason will be visiting a famous costume designer friend of hers in Arizona, who apparently has rooms and rooms full of elegant, perfect costumes. So Ms. Mason decided to measure all the boys in the cast before she left, to see if there's anything in Arizona that would be appropriate for our show.

Now, I know, Hermia has been teasing me about this nigh incessantly for a week, but it's really not even remotely as scandalous as it sounds. Usually the actors just come in and tell us what their measurements are, including shoe size and all that, and sometimes Ms. Mason does an extra measurement if there's something they don't know, or she has them try something on, while I sit there and write everything down. (Well, normally there are plenty of girls who help with *this, but this year most of them are boycotting the production in outrage over the patriarchal oppression of their rights, or whatnot.)*

In any case, Ms. Mason is there the whole time and I don't have to go anywhere near the boys with a tape measure, so it's all very innocent. But I will confess that the thought of being in the dressing room, so close to Dmitri, with an opportunity to speak to him about something other than calculus homework (a subject that has thus far mysteriously failed to draw him out)—well, it all seemed like more of fate's obvious attempts to bring us together, and I myself am not one to resist fate when it evidently has such a clear and brilliant plan.

I went straight to the dressing room after school and started organizing it for Ms. Mason: a notebook for me to write the measurements in, a screen for the boys to change behind if that became necessary, the tape measure laid out on the counter, and space cleared in the center of the room. As I was in the middle of this process, there was a rap on the door, and before I could get over to answer it, the door opened and in walked . . .

Dmitri.

I nearly fainted with surprise—I was sure he was scheduled to be third, not first—but I managed to look as unperturbed and dignified as ever, I thought. A sideways glance at the mirror assured me that despite an inadequate

amount of preparation time, I looked about
as elegant as one could reasonably expect, all
things considered. I don't even want to begin to
describe how long it took to select my outfit that
morning, but I thought the knee-length black
skirt, tall black boots, and sky-blue sweater that
perfectly brings out the color in my eyes was the
ideal combination for my first in-depth
encounter with the man of my dreams.

There was a pause. He stared at me for a
second, and I wondered if he was finally finally
feeling the forces of destiny—the undeniable surge
of connection between us. Perhaps he was thinking:
"It's her! At last! Helena, the soul mate I've been
waiting for! Why didn't I notice that when I spoke
to her at the library two weeks ago!" I was
perilously close to saying (musically):"Yes, I know, I
feel it, too," when he said, rather briskly:"Oh, hey.
From the library, right? You the costume girl?"

I blinked, taken quite off guard. The costume
girl? What happened to destiny, love, inspiration?
Couldn't he hear the celestial music swelling all
around us?

"Well? I'm here for the fitting thing. Can we
get this over with?"

I regret to record that at this point the
cleverest thing I could come up with to say was
as follows:"Um."

Luckily, just then Ms. Mason came striding in
and took over in that commanding way she has.
I sought refuge in scribbling notes, resolutely

*avoiding Dmitri's eyes. If he was going to play
hard to get, I was certainly not about to play
along. I am not the chaser! I am the chasee! There
is nothing elegant about pursuing someone, and
I'm not about to start now, thank you very much.
He could just witness my aloofness and suffer in
his solitude for all I cared.*

*"All right," Ms. Mason barked. "That's almost
everything. Why don't you try on this tunic, and
then we'll be through with you."*

*Dmitri regarded the velvet monstrosity she
handed him and heaved an aggrieved sigh, but
he took it and retreated behind the screen without
arguing. Ms. Mason tends to have that effect on
people.*

*He had just disappeared behind the screen
when there was a knock on the door. Ms. Mason
called out, "Come in!" and Alex popped his head
inside.*

*"Oh, hello Polly, I'm looking for—Helena!
There you are. Hey, what's up?"*

*"Not much, Alex." I managed a brave smile,
although inside I was still contemplating the
wreckage of my Dmitri dreams.*

*"Have you seen Hermia?" he asked. Of course.
Could he possibly be any crazier about her? It's
unfathomable to me why he hasn't done
anything about it yet, but those two aren't the
types to be swept away by love, it seems.*

*"I think she had to go straight home today,"
I said. "Her dad's being all crazy because he*

knows she's going to be spending the next two weeks with her mom, and so he's doing the overbearing protective thing while he can. We probably won't get to see her much before she leaves."

"Oh." Disappointment flitted across his face. "Ok. Well, I'll be painting for a while, so if I'm still here when you're done, want me to walk you home?"

"Sure," I said, somewhat surprised. We don't normally hang out without Hermia; I mean, he's perfectly nice and all, but all we ever have to talk about is, well, Hermia. (As it turns out, that's why he walked me home—to talk about her—but more on that later.)

"Great," he said. "Oh, and hey, do you remember what day junior prom is?"

"Right at the end of school, I think," I said. "June sixth, maybe?"

"Hmmmmm," he said.

"Are you coming to my party this weekend?" I asked—and I should perhaps confess that a part of me was hoping a certain personage ensconced behind the screen was listening. Perhaps he could benefit from a reminder, after all.

"Miss a shindig at the House of Naples?" Alex joked. "Not for the world! I'll totally be there."

"Great," I said.

"Ok, see ya." He waved at Ms. Mason and vanished.

Dmitri emerged from behind the screen and I looked up to find his (beautiful, amazing, *soulful) brown eyes studying me intently.*

"Was that Alex Sanders?" he said.

"Yes," I replied, wondering if he could hear my heart thudding away like mad.

"Did he say something about Naples?" he asked.

"My last name," I said as casually as possible, rather appalled at my inability to formulate complete sentences while he was standing so close to me.

"You mean, as in Darren Naples? The wealthiest man in Athenwood?"

"That's my dad," I said ruefully. "Or so he claims in the occasional postcard he sends me from exotic international locations."

Dmitri was looking thoughtful, as if he were about to say something, when Ms. Mason interrupted.

"Oh good Lord. This is never going to work. I don't know how those blasted Elizabethans managed it! Almost everyone looks ridiculous in this style. And you would think that of all these boys, you'd be the one most likely to look smart in any getup."

If pressed, I would have to admit that he did look pretty silly. Also uncomfortable, awkward, and scowling. Although Ms. Mason's half-compliment seemed to cheer him up a bit.

"Theo is really keen on this production being as Elizabethan as possible," I explained to him. "Including all the costumes."

"Lucky us," Ms. Mason snorted. "All right, take the wretched thing off and go back to rehearsal. Helena, I'm going to get some coffee, since I'm clearly going to need it for this. If the next boy comes in, start writing his information down. I'll be back in a moment." She stomped out the door, letting it bang shut behind her.

"She's always like that," I said into the awkward silence following her departure. "It's just the way she is, but really, I think she kind of loves the whole challenge of it, however grumpy she seems." He turned his (deep, penetrating, remarkable) eyes to me for a second, then went back behind the screen to change.

There was a pause. I fiddled with my notebook. He came out again, buttoning up his shirt, and stopped next to where I was sitting on the counter. I suddenly discovered that I was having significant trouble breathing.

"Helena, right?" he suddenly said. I glanced up, then quickly (and, I hope, beguilingly) back down again.

"That's right," I said, flipping my hair nonchalantly over my shoulder.

"You're having that party this weekend." He REMEMBERED! I mean, yes, I helped, but he did know who I was! He got my name right and everything! Maybe there was hope for us after all!

"Oh? I mean, oh, yes. Are you planning to attend?" I tilted my head charmingly at him, although I suspect the effect was somewhat *ruined by my startled expression when he suddenly seized my hand, which I was about to use to tuck my hair adorably behind my ear. I watched, astonished, as he bowed and kissed it (my hand, not my ear).*

"I wouldn't miss it for the world," he said gallantly, and with one more piercing glance, he strolled out of the dressing room.

What on earth? Where did that miraculous transformation come from? I had a sudden mental image of destiny swooping down and smacking him over the head, but one would think something would have to happen *to have that kind of effect.*

I was still staring at the door in shock when there was another knock. Was it Dmitri returning to confess his love? Or at least explain his bizarre behavior? I rearranged myself elegantly and called out, "Come in."

The doorknob turned one way, then the other, and then rattled ferociously for a minute before the door finally burst open and Nick Weaver blundered in. He barely had a second to register my presence before he tripped and nearly fell. It's really the strangest thing, that boy—he can't be in a room with me for half a minute before he turns bright red, and then he gets this blustering, sort of obnoxious attitude. Is he STILL embarrassed about eighth grade? Doesn't that seem rather absurd?

Or, as I tend to surmise, it's possible that he

just hates me. I'm not sure if I've recorded this here, dear diary, but Chrissy Canton told me once that she overheard Nick telling his friends that I'm a stuck-up snob. Can you imagine? Me? Just because at age thirteen I didn't feel like wasting my time on an inconsequential relationship, I hardly think that makes me stuck-up! Anyway, Nick is much bigger and extremely popular now, at least with the football/cheerleader crowd, so we hardly even travel in the same circles, and we certainly don't have any of the same friends.

Seeing Nick in the dressing room—in my *dressing room—was really very strange. He seemed to tower over the racks of clothes. He has gotten a lot taller since eighth grade, and even then he was the only guy in school who was taller than me. I had a hard time adjusting to the idea that he'd be changing in here, starring in my play, while I sat around watching. It felt a little like he'd invaded my space, you know?*

So I suppose I didn't give him the most friendly welcome, but all things considered, I think I was fairly civil. I mean, I had been hoping for Dmitri, after all—is it any wonder I wound up sounding a little disappointed?

"Oh. Nick."

"Helena," he said, a little stiffly. "Hoping I was someone else?"

I rolled my eyes. "Ok, way to be defensive already," I said.

"I'm not—" He stopped himself. "Look, I'm just here for the costume thing, ok? Then I'll get back out of your life."

"Hardly," I said, standing up and heading for Ms. Mason's clipboard. "As long as you're taking over my theater, you're sort of unavoidably taking over my life." I reached past him to pick up Ms. Mason's notes and he jumped back about a foot, with this weird look on his face.

"Your *theater*?" he snorted. "Are you offended by my presence here? Do you think football players aren't smart enough to be actors?"

"I *know* you *are* smart, Nick." I sighed, pointedly leaving out his friends. "Acting isn't about brains, though. It's about your heart and soul. And I have no idea what your heart and soul are suddenly doing in the theater."

"I'm going to be a great Romeo," he declared. "Wait and see. I'll be the kind of Romeo that makes the whole audience cry." See what I mean about the blustering? As if I care, since I won't be up there on stage getting embarrassed along with him.

"Yeah," I said. "I'm sure the audience will just drown in sorrow when Frank tries to follow you to the grave by kissing the poison off your lips. That won't be funny at all."

Nick blanched, but he pressed on. "They should have cast me as Juliet, too," he joked (not very amusingly). "I could just play all these parts and we'd save on the costumes."

"Ha-ha," I said. "Now tell me your

measurements and get back to rehearsal."

He pulled out a list and read them off
as I wrote them into Ms. Mason's charts. I
couldn't help noticing that his biceps are about
twice as big around as Dmitri's, and he's also
about five inches taller. Then I wondered if
it was wrong of me to even think about
comparisons like that, but I reminded myself
firmly that I am not attracted to such things.
I would much prefer a guy who is sensitive and
poetic than one with perfect upper arms, and
there's certainly no danger of me abandoning
my soul mate for someone who hates me,
anyway. It was merely a professional, scientific
observation.

I was surprised that Ms. Mason wasn't back
already when Nick finished, but I didn't want to
keep him there any longer than I had to, so I set
the notebook down and said, "All right, that's it.
Thanks for coming."

He flushed a slightly deeper red and looked
down at his hands.

"Listen, Helena—," he said. "I just wanted ...
wanted to say I'm sorry."

"Sorry?" I said. "For what?" For not speaking
to me since eighth grade? I wondered. Or for
calling me a snob? Did he know I knew about
that?

"Sorry that you're not Juliet," he mumbled.
"Because you would have been really perfect."

Then, before I could respond, he stuffed

his measurements list back in his pocket and bolted out the door.

So all in all, a very strange day, don't you agree? First, my soul mate apparently fails to recognize me, only to abruptly whip out gestures of excessive attentiveness. Then the guy who's hated and avoided me for years actually musters something closely resembling a compliment. I mean, I didn't know how seriously to take it when he said that in front of the cast list, but he wouldn't say it directly to me unless he meant it, would he?

And to top it all off, Ms. Mason revealed to me, after she returned, that the all-male cast had been her idea! Well, she had been more-or-less joking, but she apparently said to Theo after the auditions that he was never going to do anything surprising or unusual when it came to casting, so why would he even bother asking her opinion. And he said, "What do you mean by surprising and unusual?" and she made the mistake of saying, "You know, like an all-male cast, for instance." Which for some reason he seized upon, and here we are, and she's none too pleased either. But she couldn't complain to me about it too much, because that would be inappropriate, or something.

It's all most baffling. I think I'll go write some poetry to calm myself down.

Helena

Speak to Me Only

The poets say
your eyes
are windows to your soul.

My soul mate's eyes
are deep
and seek to make me whole.

His eyes confess
he loves
with passion strong and true.

I shall leap in
with faith
to give my soul to you.

Date: Sunday 16 March 11:29:00
From: AmazonGrrrl! [HermiaJ@athenwood.edu]
To: Poetess [HelenaN@athenwood.edu]
Subject: Hooray for spring break!

Helena!

Look! I found a computer! An honest-to-goodness computer, with Internet access and everything! And here I thought I'd have to spend my two weeks of spring break in a technological wasteland. ☺

Mom says I'm not to spend all my time on it, since I'm

supposed to be connecting with artists and learning what it's like to devote your life to your art and possibly also throwing some pots. (I'm almost positive that's what she said—isn't that weird? Wouldn't you think that would be kind of a destructive activity for these types of people? Artists are so odd.)

I haven't told her that my idea of "devoting my life to my art" involves a lot more in the way of swanky hotels, flashing cameras, and fabulous outfits. Or that theater is the kind of art you can't exactly go off to a colony to do—it kinda needs one of them audience things. Still, it's pretty cool here. Everyone is really intense about their work, or else they're lying on the couches in the common room bemoaning their "lack of inspiration." *hee hee*

Anyway, I had to e-mail you because all I could think about last night was how woebegone I was that I was missing your party! You better e-mail me AT ONCE to tell me all about it, you hear?

Dad did his whole crazy-person thing again, of course, when Mom and Olivia showed up. Plus he decided to tell me *as I'm getting in the car* that oh, by the way, some guy named Alex stopped by looking for me, so I should make sure to call him when I get back or something. What? In TWO WEEKS? What if it's important? What if he was suddenly seized with an urgent need to throw caution to the winds and ask me out? What if he CHANGES HIS MIND while I'm gone? AARRRRRRGH!

Well, not much I can do about it now. I mean, I sent Alex an e-mail, but you know how he is about remembering to check. And PHONES are STRICTLY FORBIDDEN here except in cases of dire emergency. Something about cluttering up our creative airwaves, I think. ☺

Hey, want to hear the coolest thing? At dinner last night, one of the artist couples told me about this show that is coming to New York in a couple of months. It sounds SOOOO amazing! It's interactive! It's outdoors! (In Central Park!) And it's all about fairies! The audience actually gets to participate—I think you have to help the fairy king and queen stop fighting, or something. Anyway, there's lots of moving around and talking to actors and stuff. Isn't that fantastic? And guess who's in it? Aaron Rex and Tanya Moon! They're such a dream couple. We TOTALLY have to go, although I think getting tickets is going to be almost impossible—it's only going to be in New York for a few weeks, because it's a Traveling Show! and refuses to be Tied Down Anywhere! ☺

Anyway, I have to go—apparently there are pots that simply must be thrown! I miss you oodles and oodles! I hope your ball was amazing and fabulous and perfect! Write to me at once and tell me everything everything everything!!!!

Hugs and kisses and orange blossoms,
Hermia!! ☺

Sunday, March 16
Dear Hermia,
    It is beyond *tragic that you are currently three hundred miles away. A letter simply cannot convey the depth and breadth and height of my*

soul's emotions right now. I need you here, *where you can explode and bury me shrieking in pillows when I tell the story too slowly, and where you can jump up and down and dance with me at the end. It's just not FAIR! Plus I TRIED to send you an e-mail and got a message back that your mailbox is too full. You WENCH. I've been telling you to clean that out for* months*! So now your punishment is having to wait for the agonizing days that it will take the postal system to get this actual handwritten letter all the way into the wilds of Vermont, so there.*

You may have figured out by now that what I'm all excited about is the ball last night. It was the most magical, sublime evening of my entire life, excepting maybe the one where you and I snuck out of our houses when we were eleven and had a midnight celebration in the woods with mangos and moonlight, and plotted how to save the world from boys and grown-ups. Do you remember that? Ok, and the midsummer four years ago when we tried to contact fairies in the wood, that was pretty wonderful too (until our dads caught us, anyway). But this was a different kind of wonderful. This was waltzing, and a long elegant lavender dress (our house is much too warm for black velvet, and I think you're right that the purple brings out the blue in my eyes), and nonalcoholic sparkling champagne, and shrimp cocktails and cute waiter-types that my dad hired for the occasion, and Dmitri. *Dmitri,*

Dmitri ... oh, amazingness.

*I wasn't really sure if he'd come, you know,
even though he said he would, especially after
how bizarre he was in the dressing room ... but
he did and he looked so charming and dashing
and gentlemanly, much more refined than most
seventeen-year-old boys. And he really noticed me,
I could tell.*

*At first it was terrible, I mean, because I had to
dance with all these other guys—the unfortunate
downside of being the star of the event is having to
say yes to practically everyone, so I hardly got a
chance to sit down all evening. And I was so
worried that Dmitri would just leave, or dance
with Somebody ELSE, and then the fourth dance he
did, he danced with that horrible Elaine girl with
the stupid perfect hair who always looks perfect,
even in gym, and then he danced with loathsome
Patricia (speaking of stuck-up snobs, Mr. Nick
Weaver!), and then he danced with Gwendolyn of
all people—like there's any of her to dance with, it
must be like dancing with spaghetti for heaven's
sake—and I suddenly decided that I didn't feel like
watching him anymore because it was simply
depressing and, although you might not realize it,
there is a categorical difference between grumpy
depression and wistful melancholy, and while the
latter may suit my naturally elusive temperament
and delicate beauty, the former suits nobody at all,
and indeed can make even lavender silk look
droopy and rumpled.*

SO, I determined to pointedly ignore him. If he didn't feel the withering scorn of his soul mate from across the dance floor, then perhaps—just perhaps—he wasn't exactly the soul mate for me after all. Of course, that's perfect nonsense; naturally he is *my soul mate, and there was never really any doubt, but it was a worthwhile experiment anyhow, as it turns out.*

I don't know exactly whom he danced the next three dances with (ok, maybe I do, but they're so not worth mentioning and believe me you don't want to know because they're icky*), but I made sure not to let him catch me looking over there (I'd caught his eye a few times earlier, but no more of that) and I smiled winsomely at all the boys I danced with, making it clear that I was devoting absolutely* all *of my attention to them (practically). And you know, Hermia, you are so right about boys being confusing. The minute I started ignoring him I could feel him watching me. Like he expected me to keep glancing in his direction to admire his popularity, but I wouldn't, not at all. This was my party (well, my father's) and I was supposed to be the sparkling one. So I smiled and fluttered and felt entirely silly and rather bored (did you have any idea that there were so many insufferable, self-absorbed, blithering boys in Athenwood?) (oh, yes, you did; you dated all of them) (just kidding!).*

In the tenth dance of the evening I finally had a break—I managed to maneuver Philip

*Greenwald into dancing with Chrissy Canton
instead of me, and I escaped off the dance floor,
very deliberately (yet gracefully, as always)
heading in the opposite direction from Dmitri.
But I couldn't stand alone for the whole dance
and still look convincingly enchanting, so I was
trying to formulate a plan and swipe hors
d'oeuvres at the same time, when guess who
suddenly appeared next to me? No, not Dmitri, not
yet. Alex! I hadn't actually seen him before then,
but I discovered for you that he didn't dance with
anybody else. Well, except me, but I figured you
wouldn't mind that.*

*So he asked me to dance with him, and
although I was kind of tired I figured it was better
than standing by myself and at least I wouldn't
have to pretend I thought HE was fascinating, so I
said yes, and we went out and started waltzing.*

*Alex asked whether I was enjoying myself
and I said of course and was he? and he said
naturally and what marvelous candelabras we'd
managed to find for the hall and I said yes, they
were wildly expensive, all the way from Germany
or something (oh, I don't know; I didn't order
them) and he complimented my dress and I said
at least nobody else was wearing lavender and
he said it suited me and I said thanks, and then
we had one of those awkward silences we always
have when you're not around to keep the
conversation going, because we both know
perfectly well the other one would rather be*

hanging out with you and we would probably never even have noticed each other if it weren't for you, and then we finally gave up pretending to have a regular conversation and we just talked about you—you know, when is she coming home (like we're both not counting the days, hours, minutes) and how his secret plot is coming along (I know something you don't know! But he's sworn me to secrecy, so I can't say anything more) and yes, I'm sure she's having fun and my goodness, artists, how thrilling, when all of a sudden *Dmitri appeared beside us.*

!!!!!

Dmitri! *Just when I'd managed to really stop thinking about him for two minutes! Well, I nearly tripped over my dress in surprise, but Alex caught my arm to steady me and then two seconds later, like he wished he'd thought of it too, Dmitri caught my other arm. So there I was, with these two guys on either side of me, practically holding me up when I so didn't need help, and I really wished you were there because I think you would have laughed like crazy.*

Dmitri gave Alex this weird, sort of hostile look, and turned to me with these intense, serious eyes, and said: "May I cut in?"

And it was so marvelous because he was asking me, *not Alex, like it* was *my decision, which lots of guys don't do (as you are always pointing out). Except I didn't know what to do* because I was feeling all flabbergasted and I didn't want to be rude to Alex but Dmitri! my soul mate! here he was! asking me to dance! OUR DESTINIES COLLIDING! so I made myself look calm and collected and I turned to Alex and thank heavens you've mentioned this whole thing to him because I could tell he understood. He looked completely cool with the whole thing and he sort of bowed to me with this little smile. And so I turned back to Dmitri and gracefully accepted his hand. He looked so delighted, I could almost feel our hearts leaping together. He sort of grinned (oh, dimples!) at Alex and said: "Well, better luck next time, Sandy Sanders." Sandy? Who calls him Sandy? Other than you when you're teasing him, anyhow.

Alex gave him this kind of amused look and sauntered away, you know, like he does, and I didn't actually see him again—I think he went home soon after. I didn't really notice because I spent the entire rest of the night dancing with Dmitri! Can you believe it? I guess his soul mate detection device has finally turned on. He's really incredibly charming, he has impeccable manners, he knows how to dance ever so well, and he likes poetry, too! And he said all sorts of admiring, observant things about our frightfully expensive furnishings and marvelously rare artworks, which you know I hardly ever think about, but it was so fascinating to be with someone who really notices and appreciates such things. How *could this not be the person I'm destined for? We clicked. It was magical. I felt like I was under some sort of spell all evening!*

So, then, after the last dance, when all the guests were saying good-bye, I walked Dmitri to the door. Just as we got there, he pulled me behind one of our potted palm trees and he kissed me! Hermia, he really did! Do you need any more soul mate proof? After pretty much only two conversations, even he could tell we were meant for each other. It was so romantic. And spontaneous. And wonderful! Although I do think it bears noting for future reference that palm trees are not exactly the ideal backdrop for kisses, since they conceal nothing and are moreover exceedingly prickly, especially through lavender silk. But nonetheless.

He's supposed to stop by and see me tomorrow sometime—he was going to a museum in the city today with his parents (look how cultured he is! And spending time with his family, too!). But tomorrow we might go for a picnic or horseback riding or something. Do you think it's too soon to show him poetry I've written about him? I know he's my soul mate, so it shouldn't make any difference, but I have a feeling you'd say I should definitely wait a while longer. Well, perhaps I will. Perhaps I'll make macaroons instead, and that way I can eat them too.

*I miss you desperately. I can't wait until you
come home and I can tell you about it all over
again. Is your vacation half as exciting as mine?
Do you miss me at all? How is your mother?*

*Write back soon! And clean out your inbox,
silly girl!*

*Love and Neptune's yellow sands,
Helena*

*P.S. I took your advice and invited Nick Weaver,
by the way, to illustrate how much of a stuck-up
snob I am NOT. And would you believe he actually
came? He looks shockingly cute all dressed up,
actually, although of course I didn't have a lot
of time to focus on him, since I had my soul
mate to concentrate on, after all. This was
the sum total of our (hopelessly typical)
interaction:*

[Pause between dance #2 and dance #3. Our heroine gracefully
maneuvers herself over to the drinks table, hoping fervently that
the significant glances coming her way from Shawn Sullivan
don't actually mean that he's about to ask her to dance. She
accepts a sparkling beverage from the classy bartender man, turns
elegantly, and comes perilously close to spilling the entire thing
all over one Nick Weaver, who has evidently been lurking in this
corner for a while, as she has not previously observed him in
attendance.]

Helena: Oh! Nick! Hi! [Yes, exclamation points and all.
                 Bear in mind that I was very surprised.]

Nick: Um. Hey. [Looks nervously about, seizes a nearby
                   soda can, starts fiddling with it]

Helena: How lovely of you to come. I didn't realize you
                   were here. [Tosses hair enchantingly, wonders if a
                   certain soul mate is watching]

Nick: I've been here. You know. For a bit. You look—I
                   mean—purple is . . . good. On you. [Crushes soda
                   can, apparently by accident, judging from the
                   surprised look on his face]

Helena: [Equally surprised, not so much by the can,
                   though] Why, thank you, Nick. [Smiles. Can't resist
                   urge to be mischievous] It's really lavender, you
                   know. [Suddenly wonders if that sounds snobbish.
                   Does that sound snobbish to you? Rapidly adds:]
                   You look nice too.

Nick: Uh . . .

[Bartender materializes, politely extricates demolished can from
Nick's massive fist, suavely retreats. Slightly awkward pause. Nick
seems somewhat at a loss. Is clearly wishing there were more soda
cans within reach. Our heroine finishes her beverage, notices Shawn
Sullivan heading purposefully her way. Decides to take drastic,
non-snobbish action]

Helena: Nick, do you want to dance?

[Nick promptly knocks over a palm tree, which pulls half the
cloth off the drinks table, scattering ice and fortuitously

unbreakable champagne glasses everywhere. In the ensuing chaos, Nick stammers multiple apologies and flees the scene, leaving our heroine no choice but to dance with the aforementioned Shawn Sullivan after all.]

So I did make an effort not to be snobbish, and it all backfired ridiculously, and now he probably hates me more than ever for luring him to a fancy event and forcing him into a situation where he would be at the mercy of his insurmountable clumsiness. I should have remembered the last time he came to my house, back in eighth grade, when he managed to somehow knock over two urns and a marble faun just by standing next to them. I wish he would understand that I never MIND stuff like that; it's not like we can't afford new ones. Plus it was rather funny. Ah, well.

Date: Tuesday 25 March 16:52:00
From: AmazonGrrrl! [HermiaJ@athenwood.edu]
To: Poetess [HelenaN@athenwood.edu]
Subject: hallelujah!

Helena!

You COMPLETELY maddening thing! I *did* clear out my inbox, and then when I didn't hear back from you I figured there must be something wrong with the computer so I gave up and I can't believe you didn't even *try* to e-mail me again! I had to wait for your letter to find out about Dmitri and then one of the artists had broken the computer for real and I had to fix it—anyway, oh my GOODNESS! Rock on, girlfriend! Although I guess you're somebody *else's* girlfriend now! ;)

So, is this official? Are you DAAAAAAAAATING? Can I say things like "Helena's BOYFRIEND said this that and the other" or do I have to keep saying "Helena's terribly thick soul mate who may one day get around to asking her out said this that and the other?" And how crazy is it that you finally have a boyfriend right when I'm single and we can't even double-date? I guess I'll just *have* to drag Alex along as my date, right? because hey, it wouldn't be right for you two to go off unchaperoned, and who else am I going to bring, and isn't this all perfectly innocent, la la la . . . ;)

And speaking of Alex, hello? Secret plot? WHAT secret plot? How DARE you know something and not tell me! Don't we have a pact or something? If we don't, then we should. I want a pact! A pact that says you have to tell me this secret! What if it's a secret plot I need to prepare for, somehow? What if I end up saying completely the wrong thing because I turn into a space cadet when surprises and pressure are involved? Can you at least tell me if this secret plot involves any declarations of undying love? Please please please?

Well, I'm coming home in two days, so I guess I'll have to wait until then to pin you down and wrestle some information out of you. But I'm warning you now! You're not getting off that easily!

And again—yay for boys who sort themselves out! Yay Dmitri and Helena forever! (or as long as you want him, anyhow) ;)

secret plots indeed!,
Hermia!

P.S. I found out what "throwing pots" actually means, which you probably already knew, didn't you? I feel just inordinately silly now. And a little more broke than usual, since Mom is docking part of my allowance to help pay for the "irreplaceable masterpiece" I smashed. It didn't look that expensive to ME. Stupid pots. At least Mom is paying for half of it herself, since she acknowledges that she could have been a *wee* bit clearer in her description of the activity. Ah, well!

Friday, March 28

Dearest, Most Wonderful Diary,

He loves me!
He loves me!
He said he loves me!
It took him less than two weeks to come to the realization that we are truly and forevermore soul mates!
This is exactly how I always envisioned true love to be!
He simply adores spending time with me. He loves coming to my house and helping me prowl through our absurdly well-stocked refrigerator. And he cannot get over the fact that we have a butler—he thinks that is ever so cultured of us.

Why yes, yes it is. Cultured is exactly what I am.
And loved! He loves me!

Yours ever so beloved,
Helena

Saturday, March 29

Dear Diary/Posterity/Future Adoring Generations,

Back in boring old Athenwood again . . . I can't
believe our vacation is already over. I'm so not ready
to go back to school on Monday. I also still can't
believe that Helena actually snagged herself a soul mate
while I was gone! Although of all the idiot boys to pick,
she had to go with that one. I mean, I always suspected
he was arrogant, but I had no idea *how* obnoxious he
could *be* until I talked to Alex last night and finally got
him to 'fess up about how he knows Dmitri.

So here's the big secret. You ready? Apparently
Dmitri is the guy who got Alex thrown out of boarding
school! They met at some summer camp when they
were eight years old, and Dmitri got all mad because
Alex kept winning all the swimming contests and Dmitri
had always been the champion. So Dmitri started
playing all these stupid practical jokes on Alex—you
know, nothing creative, just regular summer camp stuff,
like filling his bed with pinecones—and then they ended
up at the same private school the next year and they've
had this crazy competition thing going ever since.

Alex was kind of cutely embarrassed about
admitting this. He says he can't believe he used to get

so worked up about beating Dmitri. But his dad is certainly no help; he's still always comparing the two of them: "Why aren't your grades as good as Dmitri's? Why did he get first place in the science fair and you only got second? Why is Dmitri receiving special honors for achievements in finance class, and the only recognition you're getting is from your soccer coach and woodshop teachers?" and so on and so forth.

As if anyone would *want* to be like Dmitri anyhow. I bet he studies *all the time*. When he's not writing really bad poetry for Helena, anyhow (yes, apparently they've already moved into the "exchanging dreadful odes to each other" phase of the relationship—I mean, that is, of course Helena's are great, but his are pretty terrible, believe me).

Anyway, despite what Alex said, I figured that maybe Dmitri has changed, right? Let's give him the benefit of the doubt and all that. Maybe now that he's seventeen he'll be less arrogant and more mature—after all, Alex hasn't really seen him in a couple of years, so perhaps the whole competitive thing is over (in spite of Alex's father), and perhaps Dmitri will actually be able to have conversations that don't revolve around himself, right?

WELL, evidently I have no way of finding *out*, it seems, because Dmitri is acting totally unaware of my existence. I mean, ok, how obvious is it that Helena is my best friend, right? And so if he's *ever* seen her around, he's got to have noticed that we spend a *lot* of time together; and *so* he *ought* to have *figured out* that he's going to *have* to talk to *me* every *once* in a while since we'll *inevitably* be seeing each other if he's going to be with *her* and whatever, but this does not seem to have sunk into his BIG THICK HEAD at all.

Today I passed him on the street—in fact, I was even *on my way* to Helena's, and he was coming *from* there, hel*lo*—so I, thinking, *Oh, here's my best friend's boyfriend, he must be a nice guy*, smile cheerfully and wave and holler "Hey there!" but do you know what he does? He whips out that distant, looking-over-my-head expression, with the mildly puzzled eyebrow scrunch, so if anyone else saw us they'd realize that *he* is a suave, cultured fellow who would have no connection with such vulgar displays of, oh, friendliness, I suppose.

It was just so *condescending*. I *hate* people who don't respond to someone being friendly. And I *really* hate people who pretend I don't exist. I am NOT that easy to ignore. And I *especially* really hate people who ignore me specifically by gazing over my head, like I'm too short to notice. Ok, WHATEVER. This is why I should wear more orange. Or big hats. And I should carry a large umbrella for poking people as I go by. Ha! I'd like to see him ignore THAT! Stupid wildly fond-of-himself *boy*.

Anyway. It was wonderful to see Helena, though. At least *she* knows she's got a best friend, even if *he's* completely clueless about it.

BACK TO SCHOOL IN TWO DAYS!!! AAAAAACK!!!!

Love and crayons and vacations and big orange hats,
Hermia!!!

P.S. Alex is being SO mysterious. I demanded an explanation of this "secret plot" Helena mentioned, but he *refuses* to tell me anything until he "irons out all the details" or something. Eeeep! I'm skeptical that it involves us dating, though . . . I mean, what "details" could be involved in that? Wouldn't he just be like, "Hey, wait a second—you're awesome! We should date!" and then I could be like, "Hey, ok! Smooch me now!" What's so complicated about that? I mean, apart from, apparently, EVERYTHING. Hrmph.

Still, secret plot! Oooooooooo! The agony of suspense! ☺

Wednesday, April 2

Dear Hermia,

If you were a musical instrument, what would you be? What would I be? What would the boys be? Here were my thoughts:

you: drums
me: flute
Alex: fiddle
Dmitri: saxophone

If music be the food of love,
Helena

Dear Helena,

Well, clearly:

me: tambourine
you: harp
Alex: piano
Dmitri: tuba

☺ **Play on!**
Hermia!

Dear Hermia,

WELL. I'm not even going to ask what animals you think we should be. A tuba INDEED. Hrmph.

Yours indignantly,
Helena

(P.S. Although I really like the idea of being a harp. ☺)

Friday, April 4
Dearest Hermia,

History this morning was entirely insufferable, so I elected to spend my time in a far more productive fashion. I have written a poem for Dmitri. All right, another poem for Dmitri. It is about our true love. I think it movingly conveys the depth of my feeling for him. So I have copied it out here for you:

Love from the Perspective of
a True Romantic

This is not flying
I have no wings
I do not choose my fate.

I soar, I tumble, I rise
I plummet
Destiny is a cannon
It propels me to you.

You are the sun
Your fire is blazing
You have melted off my wings
And you are all I can see ...

Isn't it marvelous?

Helena

Most Brilliant and Wonderful Helena,

I adore you madly. You are my best friend in the whole
wide world. And you know I love your poems and think
you're a poetic genius and have always told you the
truth about loving them. Thus, I think it only fair that I
be perfectly honest with you and tell you that that is
without a doubt the worst poem you have ever written.
I'm afraid Dmitri's horrendous style is wearing off on

you. I had no idea that bad poetry was contagious, but as it seems to be, I think we should take drastic measures and remove you from his presence for the duration of one entire Saturday, during which you hang out with me and we read lots of decent poetry like Ogden Nash and Shakespeare until you come to your senses. But I still adore you madly!

Hermia!

P.S. Hey, maybe you should date someone else.

P.P.S. Just kidding.

P.P.P.S. Well, mostly. ☺

Hermia,

As it happens, I have plans with Dmitri this Saturday that I have no intention of breaking in order to spend time with someone who doesn't appreciate either the creative outpourings of my heart or the importance of my soul mate.

Helena

Oh Helena,

Don't be mad. I'm sorry I criticized your poem. I think it's really sweet. You know I'm not into "angst" poetry. But I'm SURE Dmitri will love it. It's right up his alley. In a good way!

Sorry sorry sorry. Can we hang out Sunday? I promise to only say nice things about Dmitri. Or nothing at all, whichever you prefer. I won't even MENTION tubas. ☺

Hermia

Hermia,

Very well. Sunday. But I expect there to be repentance cookies.

Helena

> ***Love from the Perspective of a True Romantic's Utterly Plebian Alleged***
> ***Best Friend***
>
> *Love can be difficult*
> *And also time-consuming*
> *And makes one do silly things like cry and*
> *   sigh and die.*
>
> *Much better to date boys*
> *Who mean little to you:*
> *After all,*
> *There's an overabundant existing supply*

Disposable, pose-able, available now
Easy to handle, not too much work
Insignificant flings with guy after guy
What's not to love? Except love?

If it's tragic, I'll skip it.
If it's profound, count me out.
All things meaningful, magic, and wholly poetic
Are far too much trouble
And take too much effort
And I can't be bothered
So there.

"OW!" I dropped the hammer and shook my hand vigorously. "I keep DOING that!"

"Hermia?" Alex popped his head out from behind the flats. "You ok?"

"Sure," I said wryly. "I figured I'd make my thumbs disproportionately larger than the rest of me by banging on them a bit. And you can't expect effective cosmetic improvements without a little pain, right?"

He laughed, put down his paintbrush, and came over to me. "Let's see what you've managed to do to yourself, missy." He knelt down and took my hand in his, inspecting my injured thumb.

I almost don't know how to describe what I felt right then. It was like the whole theater faded away—the other painters on the flats, Polly in the seats with Helena going over costume and prop lists, even the rehearsal in the lobby at the back, where you could hear Nick Weaver yelling

"Villain am I none!" and Pete Quincey hollering back "Turn and draw, jackass!" and Mr. Duke anxiously trying to get them to stick to the script. That all disappeared when Alex took my hand. I felt for a second like I couldn't breathe.

His eyes met mine, and suddenly I was positive, completely positive, that he was about to kiss me.

"Perhaps I can help," said a voice above us suddenly. We both started, and Alex dropped my hand. I looked up to find, of all people, Dmitri Fancy-Pants I'm-Too-Good-To-Speak-To-Techies Gilbert staring down at me.

"*You*?" I said, perhaps a little more incredulously than I meant to.

"Shouldn't you be rehearsing right now, Gilbert?" Alex said, and I don't think I was imagining the hostility in his voice either.

"I just died." Dmitri smirked. "Theo said I should come help with the set. I'm great with a hammer," he said to me with what he probably assumed was a charming grin, but I was in no mood to be charmed by this interrupting lowlife.

"I bet *Helena* could use some help," I said pointedly. She looked up when she heard her name, and spotted Dmitri onstage with us. Her face lit up into the most beautiful smile. I've never seen her look at a guy that way before. It was so cute; I would *love* it if someone was ever that obviously happy to see me! But Dmitri didn't even seem to notice. He gave her a halfhearted wave and turned back to me.

"Costumes," he scoffed. "I'm more of a power tools kind of guy. Isn't there something around here that I could drill?"

"I think your head could use a few more holes in it," Alex snapped. I gave him a surprised look. Alex almost never gets angry, and I thought he said he was over the whole competition thing with Dmitri. Maybe he felt bad for Helena, too?

"Dmitri," Helena called musically from the edge of the stage. "Do you have your car here today? Ms. Mason has some errands she said we could run together." She smiled and flipped her hair back in that way she does when she's feeling particularly self-conscious.

Dmitri and Alex glared at each other for a moment, and then Dmitri turned and strode over to Helena, leaping off the edge of the stage.

"Fine. Let's go," he said. He glanced at us again and then offered his arm to Helena, gracing her with his "charming grin." She turned pink, and they swept out of the theater without another word.

"Jeez," I said. "What was that all about?"

"Like I said, he's a jerk," Alex said, shrugging.

"Well, now he's Helena's jerk," I said, "so we should probably try to get along with him."

"Blech," said Alex, putting on his little-kid face. "Do I *hafta*?"

"Yes you do, young man," I replied sternly. "Who knows how long this foolishness is going to last? If we try to fight it, it's only going to get worse. You know that. Besides, if you're good, I'll give you all my extra pear jelly beans."

He looked indignant. "Don't you already do that?"

"Yeah, ok," I admitted. "But I could always withhold them if you don't behave."

"Yes, ma'am," he said, rolling his eyes. "Hey, are you going to be home tomorrow night?"

"On a Wednesday night? Where else would I be? Apart from here, were I actually *in* the play and thus rehearsing, but noooo."

"Ah," he said. "So I could maybe . . . stop by?"

My pulse shot through the roof. "I guess, if you want to,"

I said casually. Then a thought occurred to me, and I couldn't keep the excitement out of my voice. "Does this have to do with the secret plot?"

"Maaaaaaybe," he said with undue amounts of glee. "You'll just have to wait and see, won't you?"

"You jerk," I said, shoving him off balance. "You'll be sorry for this one day, I swear."

He just grinned evilly and went back to painting. I picked up the hammer again, consumed with curiosity. What on earth was he planning?

Tuesday, April 15

Dear Diary,

My friend Hermia does not understand love. My friend Hermia is a flibbertigibbet. My friend Hermia says that she has been in love SIX TIMES already. I do not see HOW that is possible. I would venture to observe that that is downright inconceivable (especially given the boys I've seen her date).

Of course, I love her anyway, but we do have such divergent opinions on this thoroughly important matter. She keeps asking me what I see in Dmitri, and whether I couldn't simply find someone else to fall in love with. As if a girl can just spontaneously fall in love with someone else! I believe in soul mates. I believe there is someone I am destined for. Specifically Dmitri, but I've always known I was destined for somebody.

And I can't explain "what I like" about Dmitri, because it's not a collection of characteristics. It's not like I'm specifically attracted to his nose, his sense of humor, his calculus skills, and his faith in his poetry even though it has a tendency to be a little ... melodramatic (but still wonderful, of course!). I don't think you can divide a person up into their lovable attributes. Or else, like Hermia, you'd be able to fall in love with anybody, wouldn't you? You'd be able to say, "Well, it's too bad about his personality, but I am rather fond of his upper arms and his penmanship, so I'll just focus on those. Hey, it's love!" I think not!

I mean, look at her and Alex, right? What makes this any different to her? If it was different, wouldn't she act differently? Is this really love? She doesn't even seem to take it seriously, not in a swooping romantic way, in any case.

Perhaps it is merely not the province of unromantic souls to understand the misery that can accompany true love. Perhaps it is only those with deeply sensitive sensibilities who can appreciate the tragedy of love as well as the comedy.

Ah, yes.

I think I shall write some more poetry before I sleep. I feel inspired by today. After we ran Ms. Mason's errands, we drove to the park and watched the sunset. Dmitri wove me a chain of flowers and whispered that he had never imagined such beauty as mine in his wildest

*dreams. Isn't that marvelous? A little predictable,
but marvelous nonetheless, since he said it to* me.

As the moon slips slowly through the columns,

*I am,
yours shimmeringly,
Helena*

*P.S. And guess who WON'T be getting to read this
poem!*

**An Ode
by Helena**

*Dmitri
you say
there are stars
shining brightly from my eyes.
it is your reflection
burning, burning there*

*Dmitri
you say
there are nightingales
singing softly in my voice.
it is the echoes of your whispers
sighing, dancing there*

*Dmitri
you say
there is moonlight*

glowing all around me.
it is love
it is you

Date: Wednesday 16 April 23:45:00
From: AmazonGrrrl! [HermiaJ@athenwood.edu]
To: Poetess [HelenaN@athenwood.edu]
Subject: Oh my God!

Helena!

Oh my God! Oh my God! Oh my God!

How on earth did you keep this a secret? I would have had to
tell you IMMEDIATELY! I'm so impressed with you!

and UNBELIEVABLY EXCITED!
EEP EEP EEP EEP EEP EEEEEEEEEEEP!

I swear I'm going to marry that Alex if he isn't careful!

YAY!,
Hermia! :)

Wednesday, April 16
Dear Diary,

    This is maybe the most exciting day of my entire
life ever ever ever! At least, until June sixth, which with
any luck will *really* be the most exciting day of my life.

Oh my goodness! Oh my goodness! INSANE AMOUNTS OF JOY! HOORAY!

So, Alex said he would stop by tonight, but dinner came and went, and I watched my TV shows and did my homework and time went by and he kept not showing up and not showing up, and I was like, huh, well, maybe he got tied up at the theater or something? Wouldn't he call, though? HRMMMMM. And I was trying not to worry too much, but why would he say he was coming if he wasn't going to, you know? Plus I was DYING to find out about the secret plot, and I figured this was kind of a cruel and unusual way of dragging out the suspense. I mean REALLY!

In any case, it finally got to be about 10 pm, and Dad was starting to give me suspicious looks, so I eventually had to say good night and go to bed, or he might have actually *asked* why I was lying on the couch watching the front door like a hawk.

It's a clear and starry night for once, and not that cold for this early in April, with a full moon and crickets everywhere. The smell of lilacs was coming in the window, so I left it open, and I was lying awake in bed. I'd tried to go to sleep, but it wasn't working, because I kept thinking about Alex, and a little bit about Helena and Dmitri too, because I think they're kind of worrisome, really, especially with the uber-seriousness and the terrible poetry and her being all defensive, so I finally lit a candle and was reading (which is astonishingly difficult to do by candlelight, especially with the wax melting everywhere—these candles Helena gave me are definitely romantic and enchantingly scented and all that, but they're *useless* for midnight reading) when *something* suddenly flew in my open window and splatted on the opposite wall.

I regarded the splotch on my wall in puzzlement. Then *another* something sailed across the room and splatted right next to it. Concerned for the condition of my wallpaper, I leapt out of bed and ran over to examine it. You'll never believe what they were: Raisinets! I had just made this discovery when a third chocolate-covered raisin whizzed past, narrowly missing my head. I ran to the window and discovered, yes, Alex (who *else* would throw candy at an open window and not notice the window was open?), standing in our driveway.

He waved and gestured for me to come down.

"Alex! What are you doing?" I whispered as loudly as I could without waking my dad.

"I said I'd stop by, didn't I?" He grinned rakishly.

"You are such a goon. Hang on," I said, and ducked back into my room, considering my options. First, and most importantly, was I wearing appropriate pajamas for a midnight rendezvous involving a cute boy and a secret plot?

Hrm. Green flannel pants and gray tank top. I grabbed a sweater and figured it would have to do. At least it all matched, which was kind of a miracle for me. I shouldn't actually get dressed, I figured, because that might be weird; Alex and I never dressed up to see each other. And he'd technically seen me in pajamas before, when we had moviefests at Helena's house for

Halloween and stuff like that.

Next, which of my clever sneaking-out methods to use. Sometimes it works to creep through the house and actually out the front door, but only if my dad is sleeping really really soundly, and his recent grumpiness indicates that he hasn't been doing that lately.

My dad is this odd combination of really protective and really oblivious. After Mom left him, he got all domineering and concerned, and did things like cut down all the trees near my window so I couldn't sneak out at night. Evidence has yet to show that Mom got out by climbing down a tree, but for some reason the presence of trees and the potential of women in them struck my dad as too alarming to deal with.

And when I first started dating, he would quiz all my boyfriends in intense detail, and impose all these strict rules about when to be home and stuff. At the time it bugged me a lot, even though Helena kept telling me that it made sense for twelve-year-olds to have rules like that. But I was such a *mature* twelve-year-old! Anyway, I managed to date such a string of losers that Dad practically stopped worrying altogether. They all brought me home right on time, and I swear they tried harder to please *him* than *me*. It was BORING as ANYTHING. And then they wondered why I broke up with them so fast. Not that I *wanted* to break my dad's rules, but rules seemed to be the only thing those boys could think about.

But in the end I suppose it was kind of worth it, because once Dad realized that (a) I was such a good girl (or *something*), (b) I didn't take any of these guys seriously, and (c) none of them had any *backbone* anyhow, he sort of tuned out to my romantic life.

So, back to the story. Of course, trees or no trees, I have never been deterred from sneaking out whenever I want to. I discovered with Helena (even if my boyfriends wouldn't sneak out with me, she certainly would!) that I could get onto the roof by climbing out my window, and there's a trellis at the other end of the house that I can get down and up. It involves some acrobatics, and being really quiet when I'm walking over Dad's room, but I did it all the time when we were kids, like when Helena and I went looking for fairies in the woods, so I have had a lot of practice.

I wriggled through the window and climbed quietly over the roof and down the trellis. Alex was waiting below, and to my surprise, when I got close to the bottom, he reached up, put his hands around my waist, and lifted me down to the ground.

"Hey you," I said, regaining my balance and hugging him hello. "This is quite a shocking hour to be turning up at a young lady's house, you know."

"I got a little delayed. Would you rather I hadn't come?" he said mischievously, knowing perfectly well how much I hate waiting for anything.

"All right, smart guy," I said. "So what's my surprise? What's my surprise?"

He laughed. "I think you'll want to be sitting down for this." He led me back around the side of the house to the front doorstep and we sat down, carefully out of sight of my dad's window, just to be safe.

"Okay," he said. "Are you ready? Are you sure you're ready for this?"

"ALEX," I said furiously.

"Okay, okay," he said, and handed me an envelope. I looked at it, somewhat puzzled.

"Huh," I said. "You know, I thought engagement rings still came in boxes these days." The minute I said it, I wondered if that was too risky a joke, but he laughed, so it was okay.

"Open it," he urged.

I opened the envelope and slid out the two tickets inside. It took me a minute to read them, in the dim light from the street lamp. When I finally realized what they said, I was struck literally—literally!—speechless, which NEVER happens to me!

"Can you believe it?" Alex said. "Tickets to *The Faeries' Quarrel*! I nearly died when you came back from Vermont talking about this show. I was so sure you'd somehow get yourself tickets before the ones I'd ordered arrived. Thank God they were sold out, right?" He grinned. "And it gets better. I have it on good authority that they're on the lookout for new actors right now. They have these summer internships, and sometimes they fill them in with people they've found in the audience—that's one of the benefits of an interactive show."

"Oh my God," I whispered.

"Hermia, maybe they'll discover you! Wouldn't that be amazing? You've got to be one of the most talented actresses they'll ever find. And it sounds so perfect for you. Or hey, even if they don't, it should be an amazingly fun show. The downside is, the only night I could get tickets for is June sixth, which is the same night as our junior prom. Do you mind missing it? Because I could always sell these, if you'd *rather* go to a fancy hotel and sit around with a bunch of awkward high schoolers and a terrible DJ . . ."

"Alex!" I shrieked as quietly as possible. "Oh my God oh my God!" I threw my arms around his neck and hugged him fiercely. "This is the most wonderful thing anyone's ever done for me! Are you kidding? Who needs junior prom? We're going to *The Faeries' Quarrel*! I can't even—how did you—this is so—" I ran out of words and had to leap up and do cartwheels around the lawn.

Isn't this unbelievable? I'm kind of in total shock right now. Interactive theater! Central Park! Summer internships! Real actors! New York City! Not to mention a whole night with Alex—it's practically a date, isn't it? This is SO MUCH BETTER than junior prom! I look ridiculous in formal dresses anyway; this way I can wear something appropriate for interacting with sparkly fairies—oh, this might require Helena's help. Eeeeep!

So so so so so so SO AMAZING!

Now I just have to wrangle Dad's permission. Hmmmmm. That is going to require some careful maneuvering—but how could he object, right? Alex is so responsible and trustworthy! And people go into New York City for theater all the time! Well, I'll think about how to approach the subject, but for now we're keeping it quiet, till we have it all planned. Except for

Helena, of course, who already knows, and I wouldn't really be able to not tell her, anyway. ☺ But she's great at keeping secrets, so no worries.

Joy! Joy! Joy! Joy! Joy!
Hermia!!! ☺

Wednesday, April 16

Hermia darling,

I must confess I am SO delighted that I don't have to maintain the whole Aura of Secrecy thing anymore; you are really quite a difficult person to keep a secret from! At least for me. I came perilously close to telling you Alex's plans more than once, let me assure you. But aren't you much happier that it was a surprise?

The only tragic part of the whole affair is that now I shall have to attend our junior prom without you! Silly Alex—doesn't he realize how thrilling it is to get all dressed up in beautiful long dresses and sweep off in a limousine? I suppose I can see how The Faeries' Quarrel *might be more your sort of event. But I had all these plans for you and Alex and me and Dmitri to go together!*

Assuming he asks me, of course. He does have to ask me, doesn't he? You're the one with all the boyfriend experience. Have we been dating long enough for me to assume that we'll be going

together? Doesn't he have to actually invite me to
go with him? I rather think he does. I rather
think being invited to junior prom is a critical
formative part of the high school experience, and
I should hope he would realize that, being my
soul mate and all.

> *Moonbeams and limousines,*
> *Helena*

Helena Helena Helena!

Dooooo you know what day it is?
It's the best day of the year!
It's Shakespeare's birthday!
Hooray for Shakespeare! Yay for him for being
born!

I intend to celebrate by skipping rehearsal (as if
Mr. Duke would miss me), renting *Much Ado About
Nothing* with cute cute Emma Thompson and oh-so-
smolderingly-adorable Keanu Reeves, and eating an
entire pint of ice cream myself.

Want to join me? ☺
Hermia!

P.S. No boys allowed. Even dreamy perfect soul mate
boys with blazing eyes.

Hermia dear,

Happy Shakespeare's birthday to you, too. Count me in for ice cream. And of course I won't bring Dmitri if you don't want me to, but I think if you simply made a little more effort and spent a little more time with him, you'd have a deeper understanding of how perfect and wonderful he is.

So can we talk at lunch about maybe double-dating this weekend or next? Dmitri was a little distant on our last date, and I think perhaps if there were other people there to talk to it might be less ... awkward? ... not that things are ever awkward, of course, because that would be absurd, soul mates simply don't have awkward moments. But still, it would be positively delightful if you could join us. And what a great excuse to invite Alex along, right? Oh-so-casually, which you are quite the expert at.

Off to look attentive about metaphors (dear me) ... or perhaps to gaze adoringly at my beloved, tra la la ...

Helena

Wednesday, April 30

Helena! DAHling!

Ok, I did it! Just like you suggested—I asked Alex during our free period, while we were working on the set in the theater. I was totally casual, like, "So, by the way, whatcha doin' Saturday night?" and he was all: "Nothin'."

And I was like, "Cool, ok, yup. Er. Oh, hey, well, if you want, Helena and I were thinking of going to the movies." And he was like, "Sure, I'd be up for that." And I was like, "Yeah, Dmitri might come too," and he was like, "So what, is this like, some kind of double date?"

Which would probably have been a good time for me to say: "That's right. You're my boyfriend now, didn't you know?" to see how he might react.

But instead I totally chickened out and ended up saying something thoroughly genius like: "HA-HA-HA DOUBLE DATE, that's hilarious, as if we were dating, wouldn't that be, ha-ha, funny, yeah, no, I think Helena just wants us there for moral support but ha-ha, double date, that's cute." ER. Crash. Smoldering ashes. Me all red. He gave me this weird look, and I decided that would be a good time to sidle off and hang some lights.

But anyway, he did say he'd come, so maybe the circumstances will end up being somewhat date-like, and he'll get all inspired by your blossoming romance, and find it impossible to resist asking me out. Or at the very least, I bet I can bully him into buying me popcorn. ☺

Whee! Hooray for dating!
Hermia!! ☺

ACT III

May

Date: Friday 2 May 20:45:00
From: Poetess [HelenaN@athenwood.edu]
To: AmazonGrrrl! [HermiaJ@athenwood.edu]
Subject: a concatenation of catastrophes

Oh my gracious heavens, Hermia, you must never forgive yourself for missing rehearsal tonight.

Among other catastrophes:

(1) Leo Sung (Paris) and Rob Taylor (the Nurse) have either not even tried to memorize their parts, or find it simply impossible. Whenever it's Leo's turn to speak, he paraphrases with not-quite-Shakespearean catchphrases like: "Dude, what's up with her?" and whenever Rob is on stage, he gets so flustered about wearing a dress that he generally runs right back off again.

(2) Pete Quincey (Tybalt) actually seems to have made a valiant effort to learn his lines, but can only remember one: "Have at thee, coward!" So whenever he forgets what he's supposed to say, there's a long painful pause, and everyone looks at each other, wondering whose turn it is, and then suddenly Pete will yell "Have at thee, coward!" and attack the nearest person with his plastic rapier.

(3) Dmitri, the very spirit of patience and fortitude, has evidently realized that his sensitive artistic soul can't bear the wanton destruction of Shakespeare's genius going on all around him, so he avoids interacting with any of the other actors, instead delivering his lines directly to the audience,

struggling to maintain his dignity despite the insalubrious circumstances.

(4) Frank Flutie has not shown up for a single rehearsal involving a scene between him and Romeo, and when he does attend, he stammers his way through all his lines as though being eaten alive by beavers, generally without pausing to, oh, for instance, let the other actors say *their* lines.

(5) And therefore, Theo has had me read for Juliet for the last two weeks, even though it is perfectly obvious that this for whatever reason makes Nick Weaver horrendously nervous and incapable of remembering a single word or stage direction, including "Romeo dies." Leading to moments like tonight, where I was lying onstage pretending to be pretending to be dead, and he fumbled through his final monologue, most of which Theo has cut anyway (like he has cut most of the play, to make it easier on the guys). Said monologue actually ends: "Thus with a kiss I die." And he just knelt there looking terrified and confused, until I finally whispered: "So die already!" and he obligingly keeled over.

Thank goodness Theo is having us skip any actual kissing! He keeps saying why bother, when it's Frank who'll really have to do it. Which only makes Nick *more* nervous, and, if you ask me, severely decreases the chances of Frank ever showing up at all.

At least the set looks terrific! ☺

Much love,
Helena

P.S. And actually, in a shocking twist, Tom O'Kinter isn't half bad as Friar Lawrence. There was a thespian hiding inside that boy all along! Who knew?

Sunday, May 4

Dear Diary,

Hmmm. Something weird is going on.

I mean, hopefully it's no big deal, but it's a little bit freaky.

See, last night Helena and I finally did that double date thing we've been joking about for a while, where I dragged Alex along as my "pretend" date so Helena could have another couple there, and so Alex could maybe get a clue from the way Dmitri acts around Helena (clues like: "Hey, when a guy likes a girl, he does stuff like hold her hand! And smooch her! Maybe I should try that!").

Only the problem is that Dmitri wasn't acting even remotely the way he should.

I'm getting this really creepy feeling that Dmitri is paying far too much attention to *me* instead of her. Like, hello, what? I think it's SO clear that he would never in a million years have a chance with me. Even if Helena and Alex weren't in the picture, he's fully FULLY not my type at ALL.

I really don't get what Helena sees in him. Ok, he's charming and handsome and self-assured (VERY self-assured) and witty, but I kind of feel like he's more in love with being in love than he is in love with Helena.

Does that make sense? He totally adores himself in the role of the lover: "Look at me! I'm in love! Observe how passionately swept away I am! Aren't I dashing?"

Which in a way makes him perfect for Helena, because she's a little like that—I mean, she really likes the whole Drama of Love—but the difference is that she is really serious about him, and I get the feeling he would be like this about anyone who allowed him to be as brimming with nonsense as he is. And Helena certainly encourages it ("He wrote me a poem! Guess what he said about my eyes last night! Look at his passionate shoulders!"). Personally, I don't mind a guy who enjoys being in love, as long as it actually seems like he means it. I get really weirded out by stuff that sounds fake, and I don't understand why anyone *wouldn't* be serious about Helena, since she is perfect and wonderful, after all.

Plus, I know this sounds strange, but he is a little *too* obsessed with how wealthy and upper-class she is. He keeps bringing it up; I have no idea how she hasn't noticed that. And he constantly asks if he can meet her father, like just being in the presence of the great Darren Naples would make Dmitri that much cooler and more important or something. Yeesh.

So anyway, Dmitri was talking to me far too much on Saturday night. We got to the movie theater and Alex went off to park and Helena went to the booth to pick up the tickets, and Dmitri turns to me and goes: "That's a really great outfit on you."

I gave him the most weirded-out look I could muster and said, "Uh . . . thanks. Yeah, HELENA picked it out for me. She's really terrific at clothes and stuff. She's sort of generally fantastic. Don't you think?"

"Uh-huh," he said, sort of noncommittally, the enormous jerk. There was a pause. Then he said: "So, can I buy you some popcorn?"

I didn't think I'd be able to ratchet up the incredulousness in my expression, but I somehow must have managed to, because he actually got kind of embarrassed-looking.

"No, THANK you," I said icily. "But I'm sure HELENA would love some." And I pointedly turned to Alex as he came in the door and slipped my arm through his with a winning smile. He looked a bit surprised, so I whispered: "Play along, ok? Dmitri's being kind of a creepazoid."

He narrowed his eyes at Dmitri, who gave him a hostile glare and turned to examine one of the posters.

"So, you want me to pretend I like you?" Alex whispered back to me.

"Well, don't get too crazy now," I joked. He smiled, and then, I KID YOU NOT, he *put his arm around my shoulders*! And not just in that friendly, one-of-the-guys kind of way, either. I had to look down at my shoes quickly so he didn't see the totally goofy smile on my face.

Then Helena came up, raising her eyebrows meaningfully at me and Alex, and we all went into the theater, where there was further weirdness, because Dmitri somehow maneuvered to be sitting between me and Helena, and all through the movie he kept putting his arm right next to mine on the armrest between us and "accidentally" touching my knee with his so by the end I was pressed so far to the other side of the seat that I was practically on top of Alex, which was fairly distracting in its own special way. Regretfully, though, I have to report that Alex did *not* hold my hand at any point during the movie, and instead spent the whole time gazing intently at the screen as if he had no idea that there was anyone else in the room, much less a totally cute girl (in a "great outfit," no less!) practically climbing into his lap. But THAT'S JUST FINE.

Then we went to the diner for milkshakes, and Dmitri started asking me questions about theater and what I want to do with my life and what I think of my classes, like he was expecting to totally bond with me, while ignoring Helena every time she chimed in and pretty much acting as if Alex weren't there at all. EW. I think I did a pretty good job of not playing along with him, though.

But by far the worst worst worst part of the night was when almost the entire football team came piling in the door, doing that loud joking-around thing they do. This caused several things to happen: (1) I got all embarrassed, pretended I didn't see them, and started talking too quickly in the hopes that Alex wouldn't notice them, because God knows the last person I ever want to talk to or about is Pete Quincey; (2) Helena turned bright pink and got very quiet, which meant she was thinking (AGAIN) about how Nick Weaver called her a stuck-up snob; and (3) Dmitri heaved a huge, aggravated sigh and launched immediately into a long rant about how much absolutely everyone else in the play (apart from oh-so-brilliant-and-talented-him) can't act to save their souls.

Luckily the waitress sat the guys on the other side of the restaurant, and for a while I was hopeful that they hadn't seen us. Dmitri went on and on about how much they suck, and even though I couldn't help agreeing with him, I still felt kind of bad for them. I guess Helena did, too, because at one point she said: "I thought Nick wasn't too bad in that scene you guys rehearsed on Thursday."

Dmitri snorted. "That oaf. He has no idea what he's doing up there. Can it possibly be that hard to act as if you're in love? I mean, there's not much to it."

"Don't be too hard on him," Alex said in his half-joking, half-serious way. "Bear in mind that the object of his supposed affection is Frank Flutie, after all."

"*I* could act as though I were in love with *anyone*," Dmitri declared, simultaneously taking Helena's hand in what had to be one of the most ill-timed moments I've ever seen. She looked a little taken aback and then turned an even brighter shade of pink as Nick and Pete suddenly appeared right next to us. Nick looked nervous and awkward and kept staring at the table, while Pete just looked sleazy, as usual.

"Hermia!" Pete boomed, leering. "How's it going, gorgeous? Can't stop following me around, can you?" I tried to give him a withering look, but Helena is much better at those than I am.

"Actually, Pete," she purred, jumping in for me, "it sure looks as if *you* are the one following *her*. Signing up for the play, coming to the diner—what's the matter, you run out of vapid cheerleaders? Were they unimpressed by the size of your . . . brain?" she said wickedly.

"Ha-ha," Pete said. "I'll have you know this play thing was all Nick's—"

Nick cut him off abruptly by smacking him in the back of the head.

"My apologies, ladies and gentlemen," Nick said grandiosely. "I think that's quite enough entertainment for one evening." He gave us a little half-bow and dragged Pete back to their table.

We had a moment of awkward silence.

"What was THAT all about?" Dmitri asked.

"Nothing," I said.

"Pete and Hermia—" Helena said at the same time, and stopped. I glared at her. Here's an idea, wench, why don't we NOT discuss my ex-boyfriends while on dates with my hopeful future ones?

"Pete and Hermia what?" Dmitri said, with more curiosity than anyone should ever have about *that* awful topic.

Helena glanced at me to see how she should proceed.

"They used to date," Alex said shortly.

"Oh REALLY?" Dmitri responded, looking fascinated.

"It was a bad idea," I said quickly.

"Really terrible," Helena backed me up.

"Totally meaningless," I said.

"SO of the past," she said.

"Least important relationship of my life," I said, nodding firmly, and trying to look sideways at Alex to see how he was reacting.

"Ahhh," said Dmitri, with a knowing smile. "The lady doth protest too much, methinks."

I gave him my full attention for the first time that night.

"What would you know about it?" I snapped.

"Hermia!" Helena said, looking shocked.

"I'm just saying—" Dmitri spread his hands in a conciliatory gesture.

"Well, you can just *stop* saying then, mister jerkface." I threw my napkin on the table, stood up, and stormed out into the parking lot. (Luckily I had finished my milkshake at that point, because it would have been much less dramatic if I had stopped to do that first.)

Helena followed me out a few minutes later with my jacket, thank goodness, because it was getting very cold sitting on Alex's car.

"Are you okay?" she said.

"I can't believe he said that in front of Alex!" I said. "The whole point is for Alex to understand how much I *don't* like Pete and *never* liked Pete. It didn't even occur to me it could be read the other way."

"Me neither," she said with an inappropriately dreamy sigh. "Dmitri is amazingly insightful like that."

"Insightful?" I nearly shouted. "But that's NOT what I mean! EW. My GOD."

"I know, I know," she said quickly. "I'm sure he didn't mean to upset you. And I'm really sorry I started it."

"Rrrrgh," I grumbled. "This could destroy *months* of careful hinting, Helena."

"Don't worry," she said reassuringly. "If you and

Alex are destined to be together, nothing will ultimately be able to prevent that from happening."

I rolled my eyes. "I think destiny needs to hurry its ass up, is what I think."

She laughed and hugged me, and then the boys came out and Alex drove us all home. I maintained my stony silence even when Dmitri leaned forward and whispered in my ear before getting out of the car: "Good night, *bellissima*." I mean, *seriously* ew ew ew! Yuck. Helena was like, "Oohh, did he just apologize to you?" and I had to say, "Er, yeah, sort of," because I wasn't about to tell her what he *actually* said, right? I can at least spare her that.

I SO don't get what she sees in him. Did she really not notice how slimy he was being? But perhaps he's like that to all girls, all the time. Oooo, ick, I bet that's it. Guys like that are so annoying . . . poor Helena. Maybe eventually she'll notice it and ditch him. One can hope!

Dmitri is a peacock
Helena is a star
When they get together
Who knows what they are?

Alex is a Labrador
A pearl inside a clam.
I'm in love with sunshine
That is what *I* am.

Cherries, lilacs, sunsets, thunderstorms,
Hermia!!! ☺

P.S. It's a good thing Helena's poems never rhyme. I can't think of anything that rhymes with Dmitri except, like, petri, as in "his soul could be contained in a dish of petri." Which seems very appropriate to *me* but I don't think she'd appreciate that. ☺

Hermia's Poetry

Alex shines
Helena pines
Dmitri whines
I bounce

Alex wings
Helena sings
Dmitri clings
I leap

Alex thunders
Helena wonders
Dmitri blunders
I fly off into an amber-rose-emerald-violet sunset
    full of comets
poof!

Monday, May 12

Dear Diary,

    I don't know if I've pointed this out lately, but boys are very very confusing creatures.

What is Dmitri thinking? I wish I knew what was going on in his head. He's been so weird lately. I wonder if it might be because I explained my whole soul mate theory to him. He got this peculiar nervous look on his face, like I was proposing to him or something, even though I was really careful to keep my phrasing in the realm of the hypothetical and not mention us specifically.

I'm not completely clueless—I don't need Hermia to tell me that Dmitri is (in typical boy fashion) kind of nervous about the idea of "commitment" and "forever" and "destiny." Who would have thought my soul mate would turn out to be such a hyper, jumpy person? If you're supposed to be totally comfortable with a person, shouldn't you be able to tell him things like that?

Lately I've been feeling like I need to come up with interesting things to talk to Dmitri about. Like there shouldn't be any pauses in our conversation, because then he'll get bored and we'll feel awkward and I'll get worried because we ought to be able to have "comfortable" silences. So I prepare these mental lists of all the things we could possibly discuss, but when I'm with him sometimes I'm too nervous to actually say any of them.

I believe that is partly how I ended up telling Dmitri about Alex taking Hermia to The Faeries' Quarrel *in June. I know Hermia told me not to tell anyone, but of course she must imagine I would tell Dmitri—he is my* boyfriend, *after all— and she always tells Alex everything, and I never object, right? I don't think she'll mind; I don't see what difference it could make to her.*

There was a pause in our conversation today while we were in the dressing room sewing feathers onto hats. Ok, well, I was sewing feathers onto hats, and Dmitri was sitting on the counter memorizing his lines and periodically staring at himself in the mirror (I think he was trying to visualize possible costume ideas; he's been very helpful about suggestions for things he could wear). So there was this pause, and I kind of thought, maybe if I mentioned the junior prom, it would occur to him that he should invite me to it, or at least start making plans for us to go. And the only way I could think of to bring it up casually was by talking about Alex and Hermia.

I said: "Oh, by the way, guess what?" and he said "What?" in this totally disinterested voice, which, incidentally, definitely signals something, to me. At the beginning, whenever I said "Guess what?" he'd start guessing all these crazy things and it was always really funny and adorable, oh now I'm getting upset—and I said, "You know Alex Sanders?" Right away he got interested, and gave me one of his piercing looks.

"Yes?" he said.

"Well, I don't know if I've told you this, but I have a theory that he's totally in love with Hermia, who completely likes him back, only they're both too shy to do anything about it, I mean, not that Hermia is ever shy, exactly, but it's a whole thing,

and anyway, finally something is happening because he got her tickets to this play—"

"What play?" he interrupted.

"Um, it's called The Faeries' Quarrel, *I believe. But anyway, the point is, it's happening the same night as junior prom! Isn't that ludicrous?"*

"The Faeries' Quarrel," he said thoughtfully.

"I mean, imagine missing junior prom," I said, valiantly trying to keep the conversation on topic. "It's going to be such a fun night. Aren't you looking forward to it? My dad told me that the hotel we're going to has this beautiful ballroom and he knows the owner—"

"So it's like a date?" Dmitri asked. It took me a second to realize he was still talking about Alex and Hermia, not about us.

"I suppose," I said. "It's hard to tell with those two. But it's not as much of a date as junior prom would be, after all. I imagine that will be much more romantic, don't you agree?"

"Hrm," he said.

"Well, they're not telling anyone yet, so don't say anything, ok? Hermia hasn't cleared it with her dad, so it's really important that you don't tell anyone. Like Theo, for instance—he went to college with Hermia's dad and they're still friends, so he would definitely pass it along."

"Why?" he said. "Why don't they tell him now?"

"Mr. Jackson is kind of a control freak, that's all," I said. "It requires approaching him exactly the right way."

I laughed, but Dmitri didn't even smile. His forehead was all wrinkled up the way he gets when he's trying to solve a puzzle or a problem of some sort. After about a minute, I decided it might be wise to move on to other topics, as this wasn't proceeding quite the way I'd planned.

So, he still hasn't asked me to junior prom, but hopefully now he's thinking about it, at least. I must have faith. I must. He is my soul mate, after all.

I just—I never thought my soul mate would make me so nervous. *Like I'm always wondering if I'm about to do the wrong thing. But maybe that's what being in love is like. Maybe there's always that aura of danger, of uncertainty—what if he suddenly stops loving me? What if I accidentally do the one thing that makes him realize he can't stand being around me anymore?*

Hermia would say that that is not *love, that you're supposed to be able to* trust *the person you're with and* know *they love you no matter what, but how can you ever be sure of something like that? Unless the person you're with is, like, a Golden Retriever, or something.*

I mean, isn't it possible—even likely—that a person won't feel the same way about you forever? Take Nick Weaver, for instance. When he asked me out in eighth grade, he said he "adored" me (at least, around all the stammering, that seemed to be the message). And clearly that's no longer the case, given that he loathes me now and can barely manage complete sentences in my presence.

I had a dream about Nick two nights ago, actually. I imagine it must be because I've been spending so much time with him working on the play.

In this dream, I knew that Dmitri was Romeo and I was Juliet. Except he was on the balcony, and I was down below, and I had to climb up if I wanted to see him, and I was climbing and climbing, with vines and branches all around me, until I wasn't in a garden anymore. I was in a rain forest, with trees stretching all around me and birds of all colors flying past and monkeys shrieking from nearby perches. I was afraid to look down, since I seemed to be very high up, and I knew Dmitri was above me, so I kept on ascending. Finally I saw the top, and it wasn't an elegant Italian stone balcony after all—it was a tree house, made of planks of wood all hammered together haphazardly.

I reached the edge of the tree house floor, and I was trying to climb up onto it, when this hand reached down, wrapped around one of my hands, and pulled me up. I was so sure it was Dmitri, but when I struggled to my feet and caught my balance, I looked up and saw it was Nick. And I realized that his eyes were the same color green as the rain forest around us. And the weirdest thing is, we were up so high that we could see clouds below us, but I wasn't frightened anymore.

Isn't that odd? It made me think about how Hermia and I used to be friends with Nick, and how he was always interested in everything I had to say, and how I never ran out of things to tell him. I think it was much easier to talk to him than it is to talk to Dmitri sometimes. However, I do believe that is quite understandable, given the intensity of feelings inspired by one's soul mate, which could easily overwhelm attempts at mere conversation.

In any case, if Nick's feelings can change, then one would assume that anyone's can change. Of course, I know that I will always and forever be in love with Dmitri, but perhaps you can't expect that sort of consistency from everybody. Perhaps that is also part of the curse of having a sensitive, poetic soul. Except . . . wouldn't you think my soul mate would be similarly afflicted? If he's destined for me, surely our love should be constant and dependable.

At this point I begin to question my whole belief in destiny, and then I have to stop thinking about it or else I get really upset.

So I should go do homework instead, I suppose. Or maybe I'll go find Hermia; I know she won't be wanting to do homework. Thank goodness I always have her to talk to when the silliness of boys nigh overwhelms me. Although lately it does seem that she's been trying to avoid the topic of Dmitri altogether. Sometimes I get the impression she doesn't even like him, but that

*can't really be the case. She probably hasn't spent
enough time with him. I know my best friend
and my soul mate will clearly get along with
each other, because it just wouldn't make sense
if they didn't.*

Helena

Rain Forest Eyes

*I could be happy
in a rain forest.*

*I could find meaning
beneath a canopy of emerald leaves
in a rain forest.*

*I could see eternity
in a million golden flowers
beneath a canopy of emerald leaves
in a rain forest.*

*I could hear the music of the spheres
in a trillion tiny worlds
in a million golden flowers
beneath a canopy of emerald leaves
in a rain forest.*

*I could live forever
singing words of endless wonder
in a trillion tiny worlds*

in a million golden flowers
beneath a canopy of emerald leaves
in the rain forest
of your green eyes.

Thursday, May 15

Dear Me,

Helena has told me, lots and lots of times in fact, that "peaks of joyful emotions will inevitably be followed by valleys of despair," but I never completely believed it until this moment.

I just had the most enormous immense terrible awful fight with my dad. He's so *unreasonable*! This is the WORST thing that has EVER happened to ANYONE and he doesn't even *care* that he's ruining my *life*. And it's all because of that STUPID DMITRI.

Is there any way to explain this? Have all the males in the world gone INSANE? Except Alex, of course. But he's special. Not that my DAD understands THAT. NOOOOO.

Maybe if I write about it it'll all get clearer, somehow, miraculously.

Ok, so, I'm walking home from school today, by myself, because Helena had to stay and help Mr. Duke rehearse again—I don't know why he doesn't just give in and cast her as Juliet—she's been to more rehearsals than Frank has! Anyway, I'm all cheerful and singing because the sun is shining and Alex has been so cute lately and the magic day is only three weeks

away and I finally came up with a plan for convincing
Dad, involving all kinds of responsibility and checking
in at regular hours using Alex's mom's cell phone and
coming home straight away, et cetera et cetera.

So I'm bouncing along down the street, pretending
(only in my head; I'm not completely indecorous—
except, of course, when Helena is there to embarrass)
that I'm a glamorous movie star and am trying to avoid
all my crazy fans and stalkers. And all of a sudden
somebody jumped out from behind a tree and I nearly
shrieked and flung my books at him because I was like
EEK! a STALKER FOR REAL! and now I wish I *had*, I
wish I'd just pelted him in the head with my apple
from lunch and run off hollering "You'll never get *my*
autograph, you fiendish scalliwag!" If *that* didn't scare
him off, then I'd *know* he has serious mental issues,
and I could explain that to my dad and get out of this
whole mess.

But no. I jumped, but then I saw it was Dmitri and
so I was like, "Oh—hey Dmitri. Shouldn't you be at
rehearsal?" you know, like any normal friendly person
would do to any other normal friendly person—
nothing dramatic or WEIRD or ENTICING about that,
now is there?

Without saying anything, he grabbed my arm and
pulled me behind the tree, out of sight of the street.
And then he knelt down, and before I had any idea
what he was doing, he had seized my hand and was
declaring: "Hermia, I have to confess . . . I can't hold it
in any longer—I love you, and I want you to go to the
prom with me."

!!!
!!!!!!!!!!!!!!!!!!!!!!!!!!!!!!!!!!

"I BEG your pardon," I said. "I could swear I just heard you ask me to the prom."

"And also declare my love, don't forget that part," he said, shaking his hair out of his eyes with what he probably thought was a soulful, manly gesture.

"That's NOT FUNNY, Dmitri," I said, snatching my hand back.

"I'm not being funny, Hermia," he replied. "I have come to see that you are the only girl for me, and I am certain that you feel the same way." He stood up and reached for my hand again.

"Hold it right there, cowboy," I said, pulling away. "I think somebody forgot his medication this morning."

He looked deeply offended, although Helena might have interpreted his expression as "mortally wounded" instead.

"Medication indeed," he grumbled. "It is plain to see that you are my soul's idol, my heart's breath—"

"Dmitri," I snapped, interrupting his I'm-so-dashing nonsense. "Remember me? Helena's best friend? I heard this speech already, when she gave me a detailed description of the time you declared it to her. How could you possibly *think* that I would *ever* be interested in you?"

Then he got all thunderous and furious-looking and started shouting, "Well, it doesn't matter what you think anyway. You *will* go to the junior prom with me and there's not a thing you or that arrogant Alex or your darling Helena can do about it. I *don't* love her—I love *you* and that's just the way it is, so stop being difficult about it!"

So of course I started shouting back, "You're absolutely raving mad! I don't *want* to date you or go to the prom with you or even spend one second longer in your company and there's no way on EARTH that you can make me and you so do NOT love me—that's the dumbest thing I've EVER HEARD—you've hardly ever even SPOKEN to me, you blithering NITWIT. And what MAKES YOU THINK I'd go behind my BEST FRIEND'S back to be with her boyfriend? Especially when that boyfriend is a sniveling, lying, backstabbing, self-absorbed, macho JERK like you?"

He hissed, "You can use all the excuses you like about Helena, but I know this is really about Alex. He thinks he can always have what he wants. Not this time! I'm afraid it's just too bad for you *and* that I'm-so-great smart-ass so TAKE THAT!"

And he stormed off.

I didn't know whether to laugh or burst into tears. I mean, what? What what what?

I decided to take the long way home, through the park, so I could try to figure out what on earth to do about all this. I mean, was this for real? Should I say anything to Helena? Or was he only temporarily insane, and would he maybe come to me later and be like, "I'm sorry, I'm just a freak, I really do love Helena"—in which case wouldn't it be better not to tell her, because it would totally hurt her feelings even if it was just one crazy random thing for him to do?

Or should I tell her regardless, because how could I let my best friend date someone who might be prone to crazy random TOTALLY STUPID things like this? And how could I explain it when *I* don't even know why he'd do something like that?

I finally got home round about dinnertime, still really confused and furious with Dmitri, but with a handful of bluebells to cheer me up. By then I'd pretty much managed to convince myself that he had had some sort of psychotic episode that he'd forget all about in the morning, and hopefully we'd never have to say anything about it again.

Occasionally Helena talks about how sensitive, poetic types (like her) can "sense" things that are about to happen. She says there's an "atmosphere" around people and places that can "communicate" an "intimation" of what's going on, or something. Well, universe, if you're listening: I for one would REALLY APPRECIATE some slightly more obvious signals. For instance, as I approached the house, it would have been very helpful if I could have actually *seen* enormous dark roiling thunderclouds looming over the roof.

But no. I let myself in the back door without even a hint of a warning about what was waiting for me.

Namely, Dad.

Sitting at the kitchen table.

Fuming.

"Dad?" I said cautiously, closing the door behind me and setting my bag down. "You're looking a bit more ominous than usual. Everything okay?"

"I consider myself a reasonable man," Dad said. No need to waste time on polite small talk, no sir. "All I ask of you is a certain amount of respect. A certain level of courtesy. An acknowledgment of my responsibility for your welfare."

Erm.

"What?" I said.

"Did you expect to keep this from me?" he thundered suddenly, his face purpling. "Were you planning to sneak out, is that it? Gadding off to the city in the middle of the night? To see THEATER?"

Uh-oh. Sudden new respect for the phrase "I felt my heart plummet."

"How did you—who . . . ," I stammered.

"Oh, I know all about it," he barked. "Your young friend spoke to me. He had no idea that you hadn't told me, since *he*, as a *responsible* young man, would *never* even think of lying to *his* parents."

"Who are you talking about?" I cried, astonished. Alex would never have said anything to my dad. Of course my first thought was Dmitri. But how did he even know about *The Faeries' Quarrel*? Had Helena seriously TOLD him, even though she promised not to tell anyone? What kind of best friend behavior was that?

"All he wanted was for me to intercede on his behalf," Dad went on relentlessly. "He confided in me that he politely asked to escort you to a dance, and you refused. APPARENTLY you already have plans to attend some theatrical event in the city—plans, mind you, that have not been mentioned to me—and he was hoping I'd help convince you to attend the dance instead. Well, let me tell you, Hermia, I'm this close to never letting you out of the house again."

"*WHAT?*" I shrieked. Yes, shrieked. I am not generally a shrieker, but sometimes a situation *requires* a certain decibel level. "Are you *serious*? What a conniving, obnoxious *jerk*! Dad, he did that on purpose. He knew I hadn't cleared it with you yet, but I was going to, I swear! He's just trying to get me in trouble!"

"Well, he succeeded, young lady. Although I doubt very much that he intended any such thing. He is an extremely sensible and well-behaved young man, and I for one appreciate the civility of his coming to me."

"For help in getting me to go to a *dance*? That's like the weirdest thing I've ever heard!"

"It's charming!" he bellowed.

"Fine, YOU go with him, then!" I yelled back.

"Hermia, this kind of behavior—"

"Wait, Dad, listen to me." I tried to sound reasonable. "He's a scumbag, I swear, he really is. He *can't* ask me to this dance, and there's no *way* I would go with him. He's Helena's *boyfriend*, for God's sake."

"Hermia, your friends' trivial romantic entanglements are none of my concern. What I *am* concerned about is that you lied to me and had every intention of going behind my back to engage in reckless, foolhardy behavior."

"That is SO not true!" I could feel myself starting to yell, but I couldn't stop it. "I never lied about it, it's NOT reckless, and I was GOING to tell you! We were just trying to figure out how."

"We?" he said, his face darkening.

"Me and Alex—remember Alex? He's really wonderful, and smart, and way more responsible and cool than Dmitri. He's been here for dinner several times . . . don't you remember?"

"No," he said shortly. "I don't like him."

"DAD," I said. "You can't not remember AND not like him."

"He sounds like trouble. Are you dating this boy?"

"Well, no. I mean, maybe. I don't know—maybe we will, but Dad, that's not the point."

"No, the point is that my daughter seems to think she can go gallivanting off to New York City whenever she feels like it with boys that I haven't even approved of to participate in debauchery and theatrical wantonness and God only knows what, when there are perfectly nice, reliable boys like Dmitri right here in town who want to do the polite, civilized thing of taking you to a chaperoned high school dance with my permission. Well, I won't stand for it, Hermia. Not in my house!"

"You'd rather I stabbed my best friend in the back, dated her boyfriend, ditched the guy I love, gave up all my dreams for the future, and went to a stupid dance because it's the polite thing to do?"

"Don't be melodramatic, Hermia. Missing one play has nothing to do with your 'future.'"

"Yes, it does! It's a really important play, Dad! It's like, a whole new direction for twenty-first-century theater! And being an actress is what I want to do with my life, ok? Why can't you accept that? This play could lead to internships and connections and who knows what else. It's really important to me!"

Dad was swelling up like some sort of demented tree toad, with his face getting all red and his eyebrows beetling together. I couldn't imagine *why* or what I could possibly say to calm him down. Surely I was making perfect sense? Surely he'd UNDERSTAND my perfectly LOGICAL reasoning, right? Well, that's not QUITE what happened.

"No daughter of mine is going to be an actress!" he bellowed. "I have allowed this obsession of yours to continue out of respect for Mr. Duke, but it stops after high school, do you hear me? You will pursue a sensible, respectable, stable career, and you will by no means waste your summers idling about with a pack of ignorant, prancing hoodlums! And on the night in question, you will attend this dance with young Mr. Gilbert and not go anywhere near this play, or you will be grounded for the rest of high school. You are *my* daughter and *I* will make these decisions. I am your FATHER! And I know what's best for you!"

"That's the DUMBEST, most ILLOGICAL thing I've ever heard!" I yelled, trying not to cry. "How could you know what's better for me than I do? I *know* how I feel about acting! I *know* that it's the only thing I want to do. And I know how I feel about Alex and Dmitri—you don't even know anything about them! Why on earth do you care if I go to a stupid dance?"

"I care that my daughter doesn't engage in reckless behavior. I care that you make responsible choices!"

"I AM making responsible choices! Dad, this is sick and twisted. You can't force me to go to a dance with someone I don't even like."

"Very well." He folded his arms dangerously. "I'll give you the choice. You either attend this dance with Dmitri, or you remain at home all night where I can keep an eye on you."

"You can't seriously force me to miss this play! It's maybe the most important night of my *life*!"

"Young lady, if you disobey me, you will seriously regret the consequences."

"Why don't you *understand*?!" I yelled. "I *hate* you!"

And I ran out crying, and I've been hiding in my room ever since. I heard him slam the front door a little while ago. He goes running when he's really mad, to calm down, so he probably won't be back for ages.

I hate that kind of scene, I really do. I hate dramatic histrionics and declarations of high emotion—but AAARRRGH he really brings it all out in me somehow.

God, I don't know WHAT TO DO.

Why is he being so stupid about this? Why is he being so *irrational*? Can't he see that this is important to me? And that Dmitri is a sneaky, two-faced, evil bad HORRIBLE PERSON? Doesn't he care about me at *all*?

It has to be possible to convince him. When he's calmed down a bit, I'll go talk to him. And when I've calmed down a bit, too. I really try to be calm and rational when I'm arguing with him, but he makes me so *mad*. It's like he doesn't hear anything I'm saying! Like there's a whole separate argument going on in his head. Like he looks at me, and all he can think about is how my mom ran off with an actress. But how unfair is that? I'm not the one that left him! Why should he treat *me* like a criminal?

Maybe it'll help when I present him with all the facts and all the details we worked out for keeping everything responsible and safe. Maybe if I can show him that Alex is just as "sensible" and "reliable" as Dmitri any day. The only *difference* is that *Alex* is *perfect* whereas *Dmitri* deserves to be *trampled to death* by *herds of giant porcupines*. ROAR.

And you know whose fault this *really* is. You know who just couldn't resist "sharing" the "secrets of her soul" with "the most dreamy, sensitive, poetic boy in the history of the world." It's fine with me if you act like an idiot, Helena, but couldn't you at least hold back the secrets of MY soul? I mean, for pete's sake!

Part of me wants to rip her to pieces, but another part of me REALLY wants to ask her for advice. She's so much more diplomatic than I am. Even if she has no loyalty whatsoever and has maybe just ruined my life.

AAARRRGH.

Oh *what* am I going to *do*?

Hermia

Monday, May 19

Dear Diary,

I believe it is important to write in one's diary as frequently as possible, so that one may record for posterity even the most fleeting emotions, and particularly every poetic thought, because even while one may suspect, as I do at this moment, that one will never, ever, EVER wish to come back and remember anything about these tragic events, one may, at some point, find oneself to be mistaken, and seeking back through the annals of time, one may be inexpressibly delighted to discover a carefully detailed and powerfully heart-wrenching account of one's most woebegone episodes of life.

In addition, it has often been impressed upon me, through all SORTS of eminent literature, that the most meaningful and enduring art is created in times of profound despair by those with truly artistic souls, who are capable of experiencing depths of melancholy which are no doubt unobtainable by, for instance, one's superficial, so-called best friend, who is clearly a creature of simple surface emotions.

Perhaps I should not have called her a lying seductive boyfriend-thief when she told me, though. Or a bloodsucking, bubbleheaded witch. But how can she POSSIBLY feel justified in being angry with me when I am clearly the injured party here?

I thought perhaps she was exaggerating the situation, but then I tried talking to Dmitri about it, and we had this absolutely dreadful fight. I tried to approach him in a friendly, nonthreatening way, I really did! In case there was something wrong and this was his way of manifesting it, so that maybe if I confronted him gently, he'd realize he could trust me and he'd tell me all about it. And then we'd fix everything.

But he was all cold and distant, and he informed me straight out that he no longer loves me, and that he doesn't want to see me ever again, and that I should stop "pestering" him. As if I ever pester him! I avoid pestering him so much! So then of course I did the worst possible thing and started crying, and then he got more angry and I finally had to leave because he was upsetting me so much I felt like I couldn't breathe anymore.

I didn't even get to point out to him that generally it's considered more socially acceptable to break up with a girl BEFORE you ask her best friend to the junior prom.

But this isn't what he's really like. It isn't. He is so wonderful when he's, like, not being evil. I mean, I don't want to be pathetic, I don't. But I love him. Am I supposed to just give up on that? I wouldn't want him to give up on me because of my flaws. We're supposed to work through these things, aren't we?

I just don't understand. Why would anyone do something like this? Why would a boy tell a girl he loves her and then go ask her best friend to the prom? I'm so confused. I want to crawl into a hammock and wrap myself up and stay there for several eons. Then perhaps I would emerge as a butterfly or a phoenix or something—some ethereal creature, anyhow, that could fly away and leave this nightmare of a town, with its lying boys and useless theater directors and deceitful best friends.

Why on earth would he ask her out unless he

thought she was going to say yes? She must have made him think that somehow. Maybe she's been flirting with him all along. She does flirt with everyone. So maybe he was confused by that.

But then, that's the way she always is, and maybe he wanted to misunderstand. Except it doesn't matter if she's that way with everyone else; she should have known not to be like that with my boyfriend. But why why why would he DO THIS??? Can he possibly love her? What is it about her that he loves so much more than me? Is she prettier, smarter, funnier, more understanding?

Or was it something I did? Or something I said? Is there something wrong with me?

I thought I'd found my soul mate, and he turns out to be such a stupid jerk. All I wanted was someone to love me! I don't think that's too much to ask! I hate him! I loathe him with all the fiery passion of my soul!

I wonder if there's any hope for us ...

I don't UNDERSTAND. I think boys are the most HATEFUL HORRIBLE TERRIBLE INSENSITIVE THINGS IN THE ENTIRE WORLD. They make NO SENSE and they're SELF-ABSORBED and CLUELESS and OBNOXIOUS and THUNDEROUSLY STUPID and I hate them all all all.

After we yelled at each other for a while, Hermia actually tried to tell me that I was an idiot for not seeing how much better off I am without him. Now, I can see how she might mistake that for being comforting, but see, she

*has Alex and Dmitri, while I do not have
ANYONE, so it's AWFULLY DIFFICULT to believe
that she knows anything about loneliness and
suffering and not being loved.*

I don't understand.

I DON'T UNDERSTAND.

*I'm never going to fall in love with another
boy as long as I live. I'm going to go find a
convent and be a nun and plant gardens full of
weeping white flowers and sad little purple
violets, bravely struggling through their poor
little lonely lives. And I'm going to weave
amazing tapestries of rain forests and birds and
I'm going to cry floods and floods of tears into
them so that everyone who looks at them will feel
the same pain I do. And I'm going to write
astonishing poetry that will break the hearts of
men for miles around, who will die miserably
and painfully in horrible agony, longing for just
a glimpse of the mysterious poetess that hides
herself in the nunnery, nursing her broken heart.
And I am NEVER going to speak to another
STUPID BOY as LONG as I LIVE.*

*At least, until Dmitri realizes what a terrible
mistake he is making and comes to plead for my
forgiveness.*

Woe is ME.

Helena

*P.S. I don't even know why I'm taking the time
out of my tragic reverie to record the following*

incident, but for some obscure reason I keep
thinking about it, so I suppose I might as well
write it down.

Scene: Backstage at the Athenwood High School Theater. Evening. The first (attempted) full rehearsal with costumes. Two hours in, about a quarter of the play has been struggled through, although we were forced to skip Act II, scene 2, owing to the notable absence of Frank Flutie, who did miraculously show up for Act I, scene 3, but vanished suspiciously when the time came to be onstage with Romeo. As I am for once performing my assigned duty, which is to assist in the costume changes backstage, there is no one else to step in for Juliet, and Theo has been perforce reading the lines from the audience when he is not skipping her scenes altogether.

Luckily Mercutio's next entrance is from the other side of the stage and does not require a quick change, so I have not had to interact with Dmitri very much on this occasion, which suits me just fine.

Act II, scene 3, comes to a remarkably graceful end, as both Tom O'Kinter (Friar Lawrence) and Nick Weaver (Romeo) have actually memorized most of their lines at this point, in marked contrast to all the other scenes, which have tended to conclude with members of the football team freezing in terror and bolting off stage.

Theo hollers for the stage manager to shut off the stage lights as Tom and Nick start to exit. Changing in the dark is, apparently, "authentic" and "requires practice." Of course we have small work lights rigged up backstage, but it is nonetheless very dim, and so I cannot perhaps blame Nick Weaver entirely for the ensuing pandemonium.

Theo: [Shouting, from the audience] All right, boys, let's hurry it up, next scene on stage! Romeo, you have two minutes to get into your next costume!

Nick: [Fumbling off stage in a wild panic, flailing fabric in all directions] My doublet! I need the other—the doublet—how did this get so—where's the—buckle—I think the sleeve is—aah! Aah! I've torn it! Look, my doublet's all over the place!

Helena: [Gently but firmly extricating Nick from the stage curtains] That's the curtain, Nick. Your doublet is fine.

Nick: [Relieved] Oh. [back to panicked] What about the other doublet?

Helena: It's right here. Stand still.

Nick: [Looking immensely flustered as I start to unbutton his shirt] But I—

Helena: Nick, trust me. This is my job. Stop fidgeting. [Deftly unbutton remaining buttons]

Nick: [Keeping as still as possible while still twitching as if he feels like he should be breaking something] Uh . . .

Helena: Here you go. [Slip off one doublet, hand him the next one. Find myself suddenly noticing muscles in Nick's arms. And shoulders. FIRMLY stop myself from noticing anything else. Instead cast a wistful eye on stage, where lights have come back on and one Dmitri, in the person of Mercutio, is striding on, looking dashing and proclaiming grandly.]

Nick: So you're, uh . . .

Helena: Hmmm?

Nick: You and that, uh, that guy . . .

Helena: Who, Dmitri Gilbert?

Nick: Er . . .

Helena: No. [Notice that Nick has managed to miss a button and moreover has his doublet on inside out, which one would previously have thought to be physically impossible] Come here. [Wrestle him out of doublet, turn it around, put it back on him. Start to button buttons. Wonder how it suddenly got so warm backstage] No, Dmitri and I . . . [Suddenly have trouble remembering carefully worded poetic explanation for the current derailment of true love's progress. Seem to recollect it has something to do with surmounting the foibles of fate and trusting in destiny. Oddly uninterested in sharing all this] It's complicated. [Traitorous voice quavers, revealing imminence of tears]

Nick: [Actually sounding concerned, although no doubt
             inwardly reveling in the forsaken despair of "stuck-
             up snob"] Isn't he—doesn't he—

Helena: [Sniff] Apparently not. [Sniff]

Nick: [Out of nowhere, as if possessed by the Bard
             Himself, and with surprising intensity] He is more
             knave than fool, I think.

Helena: [As close to flummoxed as I have EVER been] I
             beg your pardon?

Nick: Uh . . .

Helena: That's not from this play, is it?

Nick: Er. No. [Looking nervous and twitchy again.
             Nearby props potentially in grave danger] I like
             King Lear, too.

Helena: Are you serious? That's one of my favorites.

[Very peculiar moment here. Nick and I staring at each other.
Thought of Shakespeare seems to be making my heart beat faster.
Most bewildering]

Dmitri: [From onstage] WEAVER, CURSE YOU, GET
             ON STAGE THIS INSTANT!

Nick jumps about a foot, lunges forward, crashes into the prop table, sends assorted swords clattering to the floor, turns to pick them up, and nearly succeeds this time in bringing the entire curtain down with him. Luckily Ms. Mason is not too far away, and together we disentangle Nick, the swords, the curtain, and the extra doublet that he is suddenly clutching for some reason. We steer him back in the direction of the stage and figure anything he knocks over out there is the director's problem.

I resume mournful surveillance of soul mate and contemplate wreckage of dreams for remaining duration of rehearsal.

> *So why am I thinking about this? I'm not sure. Nick Weaver, quoting King Lear? Will wonders never cease?*

> ### The Blazon of My Love

> *Red, crimson, scarlet, red*
> *why are these the colors of love?*
> *shades of burning*
> *shades of anger*
> *wounds and flames and fury and heat—*
> *consuming.*

> *Nor is it true to paint love pink*
> *bubblegum, Barbie doll, candy-floss sweet*
> *shades of sugar*
> *shades of innocence*
> *petals and tutus and lies and lace—*
> *ornamenting.*

I wish for love that's green
emerald, oceans, cool like jade
shades of growing
shades of peace
trees and seas and belief and eternity—
healing.

Date: Friday 23 May 19:26:00
From: AmazonGrrrl! [HermiaJ@athenwood.edu]
To: Poetess [HelenaN@athenwood.edu]
Subject: the end of the world, more or less

Helena,

I can't take it. I can't take any more of us not talking to each other. It's too awful and awkward and even Polly noticed and told me to "snap out of it this instant because we have a play to put on, sunshine."

I'm sorry I yelled at you. I don't really think you're pathetic, or whining, or obsessed. Well, maybe obsessed, but in a good way, right? I mean, I think it's cool that you can love somebody that much. Too bad he doesn't deserve you. And I don't really want you to get five thousand paper cuts and then drown in lemonade. That's just how I talk when I get mad. Dmitri, however, I think deserves a much worse fate. Something involving fire ants.

I know you probably don't really want to see me, but I'm kind of in trouble, and I need some smart-girl advice, and I so wish

I could talk to you about it. I mean, I'm trying to be upbeat and hope for the best, but my campaign to convince my dad is really not working. And Mom's off on another artists' retreat in, like, Spain, so I can't even get in touch with her in time to see if she can help me.

Dad's being illogical and stubborn and won't even listen to me. Tonight he suddenly produced a new weapon, and I'm not sure how seriously to take it, or whether I should be totally freaking out.

I was in the kitchen, scraping the last of the peanut butter from the jar (one thrilling part of our little war is that I've been refusing to cook for the last few days, and he's been refusing to do the grocery shopping. I'm not sure how STARVING ourselves is supposed to help the situation, but he started it, for pete's sake. And at least I can go to Alex's for dinner if I need to; I assume Dad is just ordering in a lot. And maybe hiding the leftovers in the fridge in his study, the sneaky yahoo.).

Anyway, so he storms in the door and slaps a sheaf of papers down on the table. I did my best to pointedly ignore him.

"Remember what I said about consequences, missy? Well, here's one of them!"

And he shoved the papers at me and stormed back out again.

I waited until he was gone, and then I peeked at them. Are you ready for this? It's a set of pamphlets and an application to an ALL GIRLS' SCHOOL for JUVENILE DELINQUENTS in the remote wilds of MAINE!

I know! Isn't that the most barbaric, chauvinistic thing you've ever heard? It can't be for real, can it? It's just a scare tactic. Right? Does this sort of thing really happen to people? People who aren't trapped in, like, movies or novels or something?

I am SO not a juvenile delinquent!

Do they even *have* theater in Maine?

So, I'm a LITTLE worried right now. I need someone who can help me sort this out. Alex has been singularly unhelpful so far—lots of lovely sympathetic noises and flinging chairs around pretending they're Dad, but no concrete suggestions on what to do.

And I miss you. Are you ok? Have you tried talking to Dmitri again? Surely he'll come to his senses. How could anyone not love you? What's the matter with him, anyhow?

I hope you're feeling better. I hope you're planning on going to the prom anyway. I really hope I don't end up in a girls' school millions of miles away from here next year, because I absolutely refuse to be intimidated into going anywhere with that slimeball Dmitri (no offense). I swear, Helena, please believe me. I miss you so much.

Hugs and "Girls Only" clubs in tree houses,
Hermia

Hermia,

    Look, I understand that you feel bad and want to talk about things, but it's really not helpful for you to lurk around my locker with huge tragic eyes and then run away the minute I appear. I'll talk to you when I can deal with it, ok? I KNOW it's not your fault, but right now it's hard not to look at you and think "he chose her over me."
    Don't worry about juvenile delinquent school. I'm sure your mother would never consent to it, unless she agrees that boyfriend-stealing is a delinquent, depraved thing to do. (Sorry. Don't mind me.)

    Helena

P.S. Besides, it is quite likely that they do have theater in Maine. None of this all-male-casting nonsense at a girls' school either.

P.P.S. Not that you have to worry about it.

Wednesday, May 28

Dear Diary,

    Ok, I'm feeling much better now that we have a plan. I mean, sure, it's the kind of plan that could still result in me ending up in an all girls' school next year or grounded for the rest of my life, but the important part is that it's a plan that involves me (a) seeing *The Faeries' Quarrel* and possibly getting discovered and becoming famous, and (b) going on an honest-to-goodness date-like thing with Alex, which could lead to all kinds of miraculous realizations on his part, like about how much he wants to date me.

Right? Right. Yay!

So, here's the clever plot:

• Junior prom starts at 7 pm. *The Faeries' Quarrel* starts at 8 pm.

• At 6 pm, schmancy buses will show up in the high school parking lot to pick up all the fancily dressed juniors and cart them off to the hotel.

• Dad will insist on driving me over to the high school, all dressed up, and will probably proceed to take photos of me with icky icky Dmitri to make sure it's all really happening. He will then depart.

• At about 6:25 pm, just before the buses are supposed to leave, and hopefully as Dmitri is climbing on the bus, I will excuse myself to go to the bathroom.

• I will scoot inside the theater, scamper through to the back exit, and pop out the door into the rear faculty parking lot . . .

• . . . where my knight in shining armor (that's Alex, just to be clear) will be waiting with his car running and ready to go!

• I will leap in, and off we will drive, into the sunset, or actually, technically, away from the sunset, since New York is east of here.

• Just in time to make it to the show by 8 pm!

• Leaving Dmitri stranded on the bus, as he deserves to be, with a bus driver hopefully too grumpy to wait for long (aren't all bus drivers that grumpy?).

• And then he'll end up all alone at the junior prom, and maybe notice how beautiful and available Helena is, realize he's an idiot, and go back to her, if she'll have him.

• And with any luck, he'll be too embarrassed to go to my dad and complain, so maybe Dad will never need to find out at all.

• Or, if Dmitri is an ass and actually does complain to Dad, I'll come up with a brilliant cover story, like that I got locked inside the school and had to wait until a janitor rescued me, or something. Only hopefully more brilliant than that. ☺

• Of course, if I get discovered and the Faeries decide they want me to do a summer internship with them, I'll have to come up with something really really clever, but I figure I'll cross that bridge when I come to it.

Anyway, the important part is that we're going! And Alex is excited, and I'm excited, and it's going to be magical and wondrous, and there's nothing my dad can do about it. I was *going* to be all responsible! I was *going* to give him a detailed itinerary and five million ways to reach me, but *he's* the one who's being all unreasonable, so it's his fault we have to do it the tricky way.

So there.

And the other wonderful part is that Helena is

speaking to me again, however reluctantly, because I explained my plan to her, thereby proving that (a) I do still trust her after all, despite her tremendous life-altering betrayal, and (b) I am in no way interested in stealing her Dmitri and would be more thrilled than I can express if he would just go back to her and leave me alone already.

Yay plan! Oh, I can't wait!
Hermia! ☺ ☺ ☺

Saturday, May 31
Dear Diary,

I might be about to do a stupid thing. At least, I'm quite certain everybody else in the world would think it's a stupid thing. And Hermia would completely flip out. But I don't think it's that stupid, or that wrong, and I have reflected for many hours on the relative merits of my various options, and come to the unavoidable conclusion that the best course of action is the one I intend to pursue.

Hermia filled me in on her plan with Alex— she couldn't resist telling me, and I think in some way she thought it would cheer me up. She was like:"so, once we're gone, Dmitri will totally notice you at the prom and then you'll get back together and everything will be totally great, right?"

As IF: (a) I have any intention of going to the junior prom BY MYSELF, on the off chance that these events will take place, or (b) I could possibly stand by and allow my Dmitri to be humiliated in such a callous fashion.

For one thing, I am quite certain that if her plan does work out, Dmitri will be much too furious to even contemplate returning to me, especially *considering that he will know perfectly well that I knew about the whole thing, and he'll be convinced that I in some way conspired to disgrace him. He may in fact never speak to me again. And what kind of soul mate would I be if I stood by and let anyone, even my best friend, break his heart like this?*

SO, I've come up with this new ingenious, masterful, and potentially idiotic plan. I have decided I'm going to tell Dmitri about Hermia and Alex sneaking off to The Faeries' Quarrel.

Except, *and this is the smart part (there is a smart part!), I'm going to make sure to tell him once it's too late to stop them. I won't tell him until right after they leave, like as he's waiting by the bus, when I know their car has already left. In fact, he'll have no choice but to either let them go, or storm after them himself, immediately.*

And then I figure if he does chase them, I'll go with him, as his, like, loyal friend and helper, and maybe somewhere on the drive to New York City he'll suddenly realize that I'm the right girl for him after all! Since we won't be able to get into

*the play, there's no chance he'll be able to wreck
things for them there, but there will be plenty of
time to wander around the park romantically
trying to catch up to them (because what on
earth could possibly be more romantic than
traipsing around New York after dark searching
for the girl my true love wants to date, after all?
sigh).*

*But see? Doesn't that work? It's not really like
I'm betraying Hermia in any way, because
Dmitri won't be able to interfere with them. And
he'll see that I'm noble, and that I care more
about his happiness than our destiny because I
did try to help him—I'm not clingy and helpless
and passive. NO. I'm simply a really good friend.
Whom he will hopefully fall in love with again,
once he gets to spend some time with me and
sees how independent and helpful and
reasonable I am. It's a very sensible plan.*

Yes indeed. This is going to work.

Helena

ACT IV

June 6

Hermia:

Who knew these secret plots could be so complicated? No wonder I'm normally such a good daughter. It's flippin' DIFFICULT to be bad!

First, there's the whole game you have to go through with the angry parent. Dad was, naturally, completely psyched that I finally agreed to attend the dance with Dmitri (as was Dmitri), although he was also very suspicious (Dmitri was not. I think he really thinks I "succumbed to his charm."). I *tried* to act as if I was only giving in because of the juvenile delinquent school threat, but Dad still seemed to think I relented too fast (what did he want, MORE screaming and yelling and slamming doors? Jeez, even I was tired of it!).

So he insisted on coming shopping with Helena and me for a prom dress, which is impossible enough when (a) there's one week to go before the event, (b) I am "blessed" with a short ("petite!" squeals Helena), "curvy" figure which simply refuses to look good in ANYTHING, and (c) what I actually want to be looking for is something sparkly and club-like for New York City. Throw in an overbearing father figure who passionately hates shopping, and you have yourself one fun-filled mall outing!

Luckily Helena is amazing and helpful and brilliant about clothes, because she actually found me a dress that I didn't feel too bad about buying (considering I had no intention of wearing it for very long), and one that, more importantly, totally hid the black miniskirt, black tights, and black boots that I planned to wear underneath.

Because let me tell you, those boots would NEVER have fit in the evening bag I was bringing along, which was entirely too small for all the things I felt I needed for my transformation from junior prom gal to interactive theater participant.

This was part two of how difficult this plan was: picking a real outfit to wear (without any real money to spend on it, mind you, since Dad was watching his credit cards with an eagle eye) and smuggling it along under my prom dress. Helena loaned me the tights and kidnapped the miniskirt from the costume closet. I myself had to dig into the hidden stash in my sock drawer (left over from lifeguarding last summer) to buy the shirt, but it was sparkly and shimmery and deep pink and silky and wonderful, so I figured it was worth it. Then I just had to shove that into my purse, along with a brush, my wallet, body glitter, and breath mints (hey, a girl has to be prepared!), and voilà! I was ready to go! Stealth girl in action!

"What's in the purse?" my dad growled the minute I stepped into the living room.

I rolled my eyes at him as innocently as I could. "DAAAD. What do you think?"

"It looks like it has a lot of *something* in it," he said, very mistrustfully, in my opinion.

"You want to examine my purse? Really, Dad. How do you think I'm going to foil your evil scheme with something that could fit in here?"

"I have a feeling you could find a way," he said.

"Ok, fine," I said, lowering my voice. "It's GIRL STUFF, ok?"

That shut him up pretty quickly. Within five minutes we were in the car and on the way to the high school.

"Nice dress," he harrumphed. I didn't bother responding. The houses flicked by silently. I rearranged my dress to be sure it was covering my boots. Luckily the last thing my dad would ever notice is shoes.

Finally, we pulled into the school parking lot, and Dad turned to me as he shut off the car.

"I'm sure you'll have a lovely time. He's a very nice boy."

"Right. Nice like a crocodile," I said, shoving open my door and climbing out.

He followed with a camera, as I'd anticipated. Dmitri was standing by the entrance to the theater, looking smug and hateful. I narrowed my eyes at him as we approached, but I knew I had to act more or less friendly so he wouldn't suspect anything.

"Hermia!" he said, taking my hand.

"Dmitri," I said, snatching it back. Ok, you can hardly blame me for erring on the side of "less" friendly, can you?

"Let's take some pictures!" Dad boomed.

Yuch. I folded my arms and bared my teeth at the camera as Dmitri smarmily posed next to me (he was smart enough not to put his arm around me, though, perhaps sensing the danger to his shins involved in such a plan).

As the flash went off, I spotted Helena several feet away, by the stairs into the school. She was watching us with the saddest, most forlorn expression. And yet she still looked gorgeous as always, in a beautiful knee-length blue dress that perfectly matched her eyes and with her hair pinned up all elegantly.

"Ok, enough with the paparazzi act, Dad," I said, stepping away from Dmitri. "Excuse me a minute."

I ducked through the growing mass of juniors to where Helena was standing, still watching Dmitri chatting up my dad.

"How'd you get so beautiful?" I asked, hugging her hello.

She sighed hugely. "I should ask *you* that question. Clearly Dmitri finds you far more beautiful than me."

"Oh, please," I said. "There's not a soul in this school who would agree with that conclusion. I'm sticking with the 'he's on drugs' theory."

"I wish I knew what it is about you that has enchanted him so much," she said wistfully.

"I bet it's the cute nicknames I've given him," I joked. "Like 'meathead' and 'knucklebrains.' Or maybe it's the part where I tell him how much I hate and despise him and curse the day he was born."

"Do you think?" she said, perfectly seriously.

"Helena!" I said. "We went over this, remember? It's not *my* fault that he's being a freak. Sometimes guys just do weird things. There's no explanation for it. They're not dependable, like us. They change their minds about who they like at a moment's notice. Just reflect on Pete Quincey for a second, if you really want a classic example."

She sighed again.

"Anyway," I said, "it's not going to be a problem after tonight, ok? I'll make my escape in a few minutes, and then once everyone gets to the prom, you can swoop in and comfort him and he'll realize how perfect and wonderful you are and desperately plead to get you back. AND by the time we return from New York City tonight, *I* will not only be a rising star on her way to theatrical fame and fortune, but I will *also* have my very own boyfriend, in the person of the fabulous Alex, and then there won't be a thing Dmitri can do about it, right? Right."

Helena gave me a tragic little half-smile. "You'd better go," she said.

"Yeah." I saw my dad shake Dmitri's hand and turn to walk away. "It's almost time for my grand exit." I hugged her again. "Good luck with Dmitri, ok? And think positive! It'll all turn out all right."

Her eyes turned back to Dmitri as I waved good-bye to my dad and edged back through the crowd. Dad looked like he thought he should say something to me—like he hadn't already covered all the possible threats and sermons—but finally he just waved and headed back to his car. I breathed a sigh of relief as he pulled out of the parking lot. The secret plot was under way!

"Hermia," Dmitri said expansively as I came up to him. "Didn't I tell you things would turn out like this?"

"What can I say, Dmitri," I said. "I guess your charming personality finally just won me over."

He beamed like he thought I meant it. Brainless prat.

"Shall we ready ourselves to depart?" he said. The bus doors were opening, and the other students were starting to pile in, gossiping and giggling as they went.

"You bet," I said with what I hoped was a winning smile. "Let's get this party started!" He offered me his arm, and I began to take it, then stepped back as if something had just occurred to me.

"You know what—actually, Dmitri," I said. "I really should use the ladies' room before we leave. Who knows how long we could be trapped on that bus?"

He frowned slightly. "I don't think it's that far, really."

"Still, when a girl's got to go, a girl's got to go. I'll be right back, ok? Go save me a seat." I smiled at him again and ducked away quickly, before he could argue with me any more. After navigating back through the crowd, I bounded up the front steps and was halfway through the school door when I crashed headlong into Mr. Duke.

"Hermia?" he said, surprised. "Why aren't you getting on the bus?"

"I am, Mr. Duke," I said nervously, thinking it was just my luck to run into Dad's favorite person right when I'm being stupendously disobedient. "I needed to run to the bathroom first."

"I'm not sure I should be letting you into the school right now, young lady," he said sternly.

"Oh, come on, Mr. Duke," I wheedled. "You know I'll come right back out. I'll be super-quick, I promise."

"I hardly think it's necessary—"

"Theo!" a voice rang out behind us. We both turned, startled, to find Polly Mason striding purposefully up the steps.

"Are you interfering with my best technician?" she boomed.

"W-well, it's just that I don't think any students should be—," he started.

"Theo," she purred suddenly, laying her hand lightly on his arm. "You know, I've been meaning to talk to you about Frank's costume."

"Oh blast," he said. "What is it now?"

"I was thinking perhaps we could discuss it . . . over dinner . . . if you're interested?" She grinned sweetly at him as his jaw dropped. While he was stammering and stuttering, she slipped her arm through his and slowly drew him away from the door. I was still watching them in shock when she looked over her shoulder—and *winked* at me.

How the—did she—how did she . . . ? I looked down the stairs and spotted Helena watching from the bottom. She must have sent Polly to my rescue! I gave her a grateful wave and bolted through the doors.

I ran down the hall (which, believe you me, is outrageously difficult in boots, a miniskirt, AND a prom dress), into the theater (which was all dark except for the ghost light that's always left on), and out through the back exit. I crashed through the door and into the rear parking lot.

And there he was!

Alex!

The guy of my dreams!

Asleep in the driver's seat.

I rolled my eyes and knocked lightly on the passenger-side window. He jerked upright as I opened the door and got into the backseat.

"Oh! Hermia! Hey!" he said, shaking his head to clear it.

"Expecting someone else?" I teased. "This isn't the most impressive start to our secret escape, sunshine. I think most knights in shining armor are awake when they do their dragon slaying."

"I don't remember consciousness being in the job description," he said with a yawn.

"Well, if you can muster the energy, could we start driving? I got a little delayed on the way, and I don't want Dmitri figuring anything out before we've managed to get away." I slid to the floor and ducked down out of sight of the windows, fishing my shirt out of my bag.

"Paranoid much?" Alex said, still grinning as he reversed and turned out of the parking lot.

"You'd be paranoid too if everyone was after you." I gave him our favorite response.

"Sorry about the sleepiness," he said. "I couldn't fall

asleep last night. I don't know why—all the excitement, maybe." He glanced back and down at me with this cute shy look on his face and then quickly turned back to the road.

I stared at him in amazement. Was he serious? He'd lost sleep over this? I mean, I was pretty insanely excited, too. But sleeping? *Never* a problem for me.

I could actually feel my heartbeat speed up, which, considering I was still recovering from my mad dash through the halls, was pretty impressive, I thought.

"Ok, we're on the highway," he said. "I think you're safe now."

I wrinkled my nose at him. "Are you sure we're not being followed?"

"By Dmitri?" he said mysteriously. "Oh, I don't think you have to worry about *him* coming after us."

"What's that supposed to mean?"

"Don't worry about it," he said. "Hey, listen, don't get me wrong. I think floor-length bell-shaped ballgowns are totally hot, especially on you. But is that actually what you're planning on wearing? I'm not sure it's appropriate attire for this kind of shindig."

I blinked. Was that flirting? Sounded like flirting to me!

"Trust me, this is coming off as soon as possible," I said, and then realized how that sounded when he raised his eyebrows. I reached up and smacked him lightly on the back of the head. "I mean, I'm changing right now, dorkus. Keep your eyes on the road, or else." He laughed, and politely obliged as I wriggled around to unzip my dress.

"What about you?" I said. "When are you going to change?"

"Change?" he said, glancing down at himself.

"That's not what you're wearing, is it?"

He started laughing again. "Like they'll really care what

I'm wearing. This is about *your* fame and fortune, remember?"

"But, Alex—"

"But nothing," he said. "I think you should be impressed enough that I agreed to wear these fancy-pants corduroys instead of jeans."

"There's no way I could convince you to ditch the Athenwood Theater sweatshirt?"

"And relinquish my school pride? No way!"

"You are SUCH a dork," I said, snapping the last button and climbing into the front seat. He glanced over at me as I fastened my seat belt.

"Whoa," he said.

"Whoa what? Bad whoa? Like, fashion disaster whoa?"

"Not remotely," he said. "You look amazing."

"Oh—thanks," I said with what I'm sure was just about the silliest smile in the history of the universe. He grinned back at me.

Yup. This was going to be the most perfect night ever.

Helena:

I leaned against the giant owl statue at the bottom of the stairs to the high school, trying to breathe normally. I had to time this right. If I didn't give Hermia and Alex enough time to get away, all my carefully laid plans would go horribly horribly awry.

Luckily Ms. Mason had come along at exactly the right moment. I hadn't had time to give her the whole explanation, but she could see that I thought it was urgent. Besides, when I said that Hermia needed her help, that was really all she had to hear.

She and Theo had disappeared somewhere. The buses

were almost entirely loaded, with a few stragglers pulling in at the last minute. Dmitri hadn't got on to save Hermia a seat after all; he was leaning against one of the buses, flipping a coin and glancing at his watch impatiently.

He didn't look as completely heartbroken as I would have expected. I surmised that he hadn't realized what was going on yet, although I couldn't believe he could really think Hermia would take this long. Maybe he simply didn't imagine anyone would do such a thing to him. I caught myself on the verge of having an ungenerous thought about my soul mate and amended it to, *Well, he is clearly a trusting soul with no inkling of the darkness lurking in people's hearts*. It wasn't a hundred percent convincing, since he seemed to be spreading around a lot of darkness himself lately, but I was determined to give him the benefit of the doubt.

He flicked open his pocketwatch again (a pocketwatch! how elegant is that?) and scowled. I took a deep breath and steeled myself. It was now or never.

He rolled his eyes as he saw me approaching.

"What do *you* want?" he said scornfully. (Impatiently, I amended in my head. No—anxiously? Urp.) All my carefully rehearsed lines flew out of my mind at once.

"Dmitri," I managed.

"Look, I said to leave me alone, ok?"

"I will," I said. "I just wanted to tell you—"

"Can't it wait? Hermia and I are about to leave for the prom."

"No, you're not," I said, and had to stifle what was almost a moment of glee at the expression on his face.

"What do you mean?" he said, instantly suspicious.

"She's not coming back," I said. I was surprised at how

challenging it was to sound sympathetic rather than triumphant. Really, what kind of soul mate was I? Wasn't I supposed to be all understanding of his troubled emotions?

"Where did she go?" he sputtered, turning red. "Are you telling me she—with Alex—that play—"

"I'm afraid so," I said. "I'm sorry. I couldn't let it happen without—without warning you. I know how inconsolable you must feel."

"I'm going to KILL that guy!" he shouted, and charged off across the parking lot. I hurried after him, which was not an easy thing to accomplish gracefully in heels.

"I know, I couldn't believe it," I said. "I mean, what a lack of respect, for one thing, and it's so heartless, really, and listen, if you need a shoulder to cry on—"

"Oh, shut up," he said, pulling out his car keys as we got to his car. This was it. This was my last chance to accompany him. My last chance to prove what a helpmeet and supportive soul mate I could be.

"I know where the show is," I said, a smidgen more desperately than I meant to.

"I'm sure you do," he said. "I can find it on my own."

"But I could help," I said. "I could get you there faster. You'll never catch them by yourself."

"BLAST BLAST BLAST!" he yelled suddenly. I jumped back about a foot. Certainly I had anticipated anger, but this was rather more extreme than I had pictured. Then again, I had also pictured more noble despair and outpourings of grief, so I was already somewhat off the mark.

He whirled on me. "Did you do this?" he barked.

"Do what?" I stammered.

"No, you wouldn't," he said. "It must have been Sanders."

He followed that up with a stream of colorful invective, through which I eventually discerned the underlying problem: Someone had removed two of his tires. Alex had thought ahead more than I'd expected.

My heart drooped and woe flooded through me. That was it, then. No trip into New York, no romantic chase sequence, no opportunity to prove my love. Not that it was going that well so far, or anything.

I felt awash in sadness. Dmitri stood there yelling at his car and ignoring me completely. Slowly I turned and headed despondently (yet still elegantly) back to the high school steps. The buses had all departed, and the parking lot was completely deserted except for me and Dmitri.

I sat down on the lowest step and dropped my head into my hands. How had everything gone so wrong so quickly? At least there was definitely no chance of screwing up Hermia's plan at this point. Dmitri would just rant and rave himself out, and then react however he would have reacted anyway. What I had done made no difference at all, except that I felt like even more of a pathetic idiot.

I could hear Dmitri shouting personal curses at his cell phone now, which evidently also wasn't working for some reason. I willed myself not to cry. Nobody looks elegant and irresistible with mascara smeared all over her face. And for goodness sakes, no matter how Dmitri chose to behave, I could at least maintain my style, couldn't I? My mother would never have cried on the steps of a high school.

But then again, my mother would also never have been ditched by a guy for her best friend (of course, given that her best friend was Hermia's mom, the guy wouldn't have had much of a chance anyway).

"Helena?"

I lifted my determinedly not-tear-stained face, startled. A car had driven up in front of me without my noticing. And emerging from it with a concerned expression on his face was, of all people, Nick Weaver.

This for some reason made me want to bawl more than ever. I hid my face in my hands, concentrating on not crying.

"Helena? What's wrong?" Nick's gigantic feet came into my line of sight. Did he just get larger all the time?

"Nothing," I mumbled.

He hovered for a second, clearly disbelieving. I wondered if he was thinking about how much he hated me, and if he was trying to figure out a way to escape this situation politely. Well, it certainly wasn't my job to help him with that, was it? No. Certainly not. Stuck-up snob indeed.

"Is—is there anything I can do?" he said at length.

I sighed, leaned my head on my hands, and looked up at him again. "It's ok, Nick. You don't have to stick around. I'm sure you have places to be."

"Always," he said with a half-grin and an almost-swagger. "What can I say—I'm in high demand. But right now I'm waiting for Pete. So, you, uh . . . you want to talk about it?"

"Even if I did, you most certainly wouldn't want to hear about it," I said.

"Oh, I dunno—," he began, when suddenly Dmitri popped up next to him and interrupted.

"You!" Dmitri barked. Nick stopped and looked at him with mild surprise and possibly a level of dislike, although it was hard to tell, because quite frankly, Nick's expression doesn't ever change very much.

"I actually go by 'Nick' these days," he commented.

(Sarcasm? Was that sarcasm? From *Nick*?)

"You have a car," Dmitri barged on.

"Mmmm," Nick agreed, more or less.

"I need it," Dmitri said.

"Dmitri!" I said, shocked.

"I can pay you for it, just for the night," he said, giving me an irritated look.

"Well, that's mighty generous of you, Dmitri, but as it happens, I need it myself tonight," Nick said.

"For what?" Dmitri scoffed. "Hanging out with your dumb jock friends? Come on, this is important."

Nick drew himself up and frowned down at Dmitri. "AS it so happens," Nick said, "my 'dumb jock friends' and I are going to a play tonight. So I *do* need my car."

"What play?" I said, interested despite myself. Nick and his friends in a theater? I mean, a theater where they weren't, like, inexplicably stealing other people's parts?

"Mr. Duke thought it would be a good experience for us to see some real theater, so I got tickets for me and the guys. It's in Central Park, in the city. It's called the fairy something . . . *Fairy Fight*? Something like that. My dad knows somebody who got us the tickets."

I was speechless. Dmitri, unfortunately, was not.

"*The Faeries' Quarrel*?" he yelped. "That's where *I* have to go. This *minute*."

"Wait, Dmitri," I said. "We can't ask Nick for his tickets." Lord, Hermia would KILL me if we showed up at her play! She would scratch my eyes out and accuse me of betrayal (again), and worst of all, I would completely deserve it. Not to mention how uncivilized it would be to swipe someone else's tickets, even a football jock's.

"I only need one," Dmitri practically snarled. Nick looked from me to him and back again.

"Well," he said slowly. "As a matter of fact . . ."

"What?" Dmitri said. "What?"

"We *do* have extras," he said. "I got a bunch for some of the guys, but now it's just me and Pete going. Rob and Tom ended up taking their girlfriends to the prom instead, and Frank is sick, or so he says." He looked at me again, seriously. "So if you want them . . ."

"I do," Dmitri said.

"I'm asking Helena," Nick said.

What could I do? Talk about unspeakable torment. This was clearly vengeful retribution brought down upon me for betraying my best friend. This was probably only the beginning of my dreadful punishment. If I said yes, we'd end up at the play and Hermia would absolutely die, or more likely, smother me with the stage curtains. But Dmitri was staring at me now, his brown eyes huge and soulful and intense. He *needed* me. He needed me to save his honor and dignity and give him a measure of hope in this tragic chase. How could I say no? Then he would truly never forgive me, and our entire future bliss would be completely wrecked.

I had no choice. True love was at stake.

"We'd love to accompany you to *The Faeries' Quarrel*, Nick," I said. He seemed to think for a second, then shrugged and turned back to his car. Dmitri snorted and followed him. As Nick opened the doors, another car pulled up and Pete Quincey popped out, looking his usual smarmy self.

"Helena!" he bellowed, sizing up the situation. "What's up? Coming with us to see some thee-ay-turrr?" He grinned broadly and winked. My heart sank as I realized that not only would I be showing up in the middle of Hermia's perfect night accompanied by Dmitri, whom she was trying to escape from, and Nick, who was an embarrassment to anyone in his immediate vicinity, but also Pete Quincey, Hermia's most loathsome ex.

Oh, gods. What had I done?

Hermia:

"Wow," I said again. "Wow, Alex. I mean . . . wow."

"Yeah, I think you pointed that out already." He laughed.

We were standing in the center of a ring of trees in Central Park, with about two hundred other people, I guessed. There were no seats, but there was a sort of natural stage at one end, where a series of large, flat rocks led up to a hilltop. The immediate vicinity was surrounded by a tall silvery fence, with burly guards at the one entrance, and the only building within the fenced area was a small concrete structure for rest rooms, at the opposite end from the stage.

Moonlight filtered down through the trees, giving the whole place an eerie glow, and a breeze made the leaves above us dance, shimmering. There were also metal arms jutting out of the fence with lights attached to them, adding swirling colors and roving star-shaped light patterns to the ambience. Speakers along the edges of the fence surrounded us with powerful, pulsating dance music. It was amazing. It was romantic. It was *perfect*.

"Look at those lights!" I said. "Do you know how expensive they are? Just ONE of those would be, like, our entire spring production budget."

"But hey, who needs costumes and sets when you've got

a spinning-color light, right?" he joked. "Personally, I think the most amazing thing is that we got here in time."

"Especially with mister falling-asleep-at-the-wheel here," I said, shoving him lightly.

"I was not!" he protested. There was a moment where we both looked at each other, smiling, and then he put his arm around my shoulders again, like he had at the movies. *All casual and suave! Look at him being all casual and suave!* I slipped my arm around his waist and leaned into him a little. *Two could play this suave game!* Or at least, I could pretend real well.

Suddenly the music dropped away, leaving one high, pure sound: something ethereal and weird . . . like an electric flute, if there's any such thing. People around us hushed and turned toward the stage, where smoke was starting to creep up from behind the hilltop. A thrumming drumbeat began building under the other sound, pulsing through the ground and almost commanding us to sway as the fog on stage grew thicker.

All at once there was a BANG, bright colors came shooting out of the lights all around us, and the music kicked into high gear. The smoke cleared, revealing the highest rock platform. And there she was:

The Faerie Queen herself: Tanya Moon!

Helena:

"Maybe we're too late," I said nervously.

"Nonsense," Dmitri snapped.

A burly man in a suit stood by the gate, studying us carefully as we approached. I had known generally where the theater was in Central Park, but I had never been there before, and it was much darker and wilder and scarier than I expected. Not to mention I was feeling almost ill from the horrendous experience of a car ride with Nick, Pete, and Dmitri.

Pete, of course, was his usual annoying self, and Nick for the most part played along with him, both of them joking about how action movies are the true highest form of theatrical art, et cetera et cetera, aren't we manly. Dmitri for the most part stared out the window, thinking his deep tragic thoughts about the state of the universe and the inconstancy of women, no doubt (and, by the way, as *if*, because *I* am as constant as the *sun*, so *there*). He only spoke twice, once to say:

"I can't wear this into the theater," taking off his tuxedo jacket and looking disgusted. Nick glanced over his shoulder and waved at the backseat.

"There's a couple of those sweatshirts Mr. Duke gave us on the floor. You can borrow one. I mean, like I'll ever wear it."

"Not big enough for the MAN, right?" Pete said, and they did some strange primitive hand interaction to indicate their, I don't know, strange primitivism, perhaps.

Dmitri lifted one of the Athenwood High Theater sweatshirts out of the box on the floor and regarded it disdainfully.

"It's better than just a tuxedo shirt and pants, I suppose," I said (Supportive! Yes I am! I support my beloved in all ways, even sartorially!) (If only Hermia were here to appreciate my use of the word *sartorial* in a sentence). He shot me a look, put on the sweatshirt, and went back to staring out the window. *Well, fine then*, I thought. *To be perfectly honest, he does look a little silly. Would he rather I pointed that out? Highly doubtful.*

The other time he spoke was as we got out of the car, while Pete was getting the garage ticket. I'd climbed out first, and I held the door open for Dmitri, and as he got out he looked at me and muttered, "I don't know why you're coming along, anyway."

"If she weren't here, you wouldn't be either," Nick said forcefully from behind me, making me jump. The two guys glared at each other for a second, and then Dmitri strode past him, heading for the exit.

"He's going on without us?" I said in disbelief.

"He won't get far." Nick grinned. "I've still got all the tickets." He turned back to Pete as I scooted after Dmitri, again far less gracefully than I would have liked. *How did Dmitri miss the basic principles of soul-matehood*, I wondered as I tried to keep up with him. *Why doesn't anything ever happen the way it's supposed to? Girls are not supposed to be the pursuers, no indeed. This was decidedly* not *the plan.* Why couldn't he do clear, understandable things, like the princes in the fairy tales? There's never any sort of doubt that they love their princesses. We needed a dragon or something, so he'd have something real to fight, instead of feeling like he had to fight little old ME.

I wish I could go back to being elegant and unattainable. I'm much better at that part. I am not even remotely skilled at this pursuing-boys-through-the-streets-of-Manhattan thing. We reached the outskirts of Central Park with Nick and Pete about half a block behind us. I jumped as a gigantic truck rumbled past, honking at a shockingly unreasonable decibel level. Apart from all the other stress, I was also positive that I LOOKED just TERRIBLE. It is VERY DIFFICULT to dress simultaneously for (a) making your semi-ex-boyfriend realize how attractive you really are, and (b) traipsing about Central Park in the dark. There are NO clear fashion rules for this.

I can't believe I'm doing this. It's like some sort of demented dream.

Now Dmitri and I were level with the burly man, who looked at us as if smiling were not really a favorite pastime of his. Dmitri glanced back impatiently at where Nick and Pete were strolling through the trees behind us.

"Listen, Helena," he suddenly said to me. "I don't want you getting in my way in there. I've told you we're through, and all I want here is to get my girl back."

"Your *girl?*" I said. "You mean Hermia? Hermia is *nobody's* girl."

"Not even Alex's?" Dmitri said snidely.

"Not even," I said.

"I don't know why she's acting like this," he said. "She knows how I feel about her. I think I was very clear."

"Like you were clear to me?" I said, sounding, I'll admit, substantially more bitter than I meant to. *Focus, Helena*, I thought. *Supportive, remember?*

"I didn't ask you to follow me here, Helena."

"Yes," I said, "but I refuse to let a detour like this derail the course of my true love. I'm a devoted person, and I think eventually you will realize the value of that."

"OH MY GOD," he said. "I *told* you I'm not interested anymore. WHY can't you get that through your thick head?"

"I can't help the way I feel," I protested. "I can't explain it, or change it. When I say I love someone, I mean it forever. Doesn't everyone?"

"Whatever," he said. "Just don't get in my way."

At that point Nick and Pete came up, fortunately, because there is really only so much a girl's heart can take, even when that girl is stalwart and true and determined to overcome any obstacle, including her soul mate's apparent severe personality disorder.

"Tickets?" the burly man said in a low voice. Nick stepped forward, brandishing them with an easy smile.

"Yeah, we got tickets," he said. "No chance we're too late for the show, is there?"

"You're the last ones here," the burly man growled. He looked discomfited by the fact that Nick was taller and larger than him, as if that didn't happen to him very often.

"Too bad, Pete," Nick joked. "There's no escape now. We're stuck with this band of fairies for the next two hours." I rolled my eyes and smiled at the ticket guy as Nick and Pete made the requisite stupid jokes. He narrowed his eyes at Nick as he tore our tickets in half and handed them back to us, but he gave me a slightly more friendly look as we filed past him into the ring of trees.

"Have a magical night," he rumbled, stepping inside behind us, closing the gate, and disappearing into the bushes. Something about the way he said it made me turn and watch him go, like there was something familiar about him.

Was it—could it have been—but no, why would *he* have been taking tickets?

And yet, a part of me had an eerie feeling we had just been welcomed by Aaron Rex . . . the Faerie King himself.

Hermia:

The beginning of the show passed in a blur. The Faerie Queen and her attendants did a whole song and dance about how she was furious with her husband (the Faerie King) for cheating on her, and how she intended to find a way to punish him. It involved a lot of acrobatics and running through the audience and getting us to dance as well. I threw myself into it wholeheartedly, thinking if I ever got cast in this I'd certainly be getting as much exercise as I could possibly ever need.

Alex was a little more restrained, but he seemed to be having fun. Or, at least, he seemed to enjoy laughing at me.

"Come *on*, Alex!" I yelled in his ear. "Don't you want to go dance near the stage?"

"Nooooo, thanks," he yelled back. "I've heard how they drag people up there. But you go ahead—I'm going to get some water."

"Ok," I said, waving as he ducked away into the crowd. Silly guy—dancing on stage was the whole POINT of this excursion! I wove my way closer to the stage as suddenly, in a flash of light, somebody leaped out from behind a large tree near the stage.

Aaron Rex! It had to be him! All around me audience members started shrieking and jumping up and down (ok, yeah, maybe I did, too). He was wearing shockingly little in the way of clothes, and a whole lot in the way of glitter. He was a lot larger than I'd realized from seeing him on Broadway before. Tanya Moon, who had been his leading lady in everything I'd ever seen them in, was almost as tall as him. I would look practically midget-sized next to them, but that could be good, right? Like I was one of their small fairy attendants?

He leaped up the rocks until he was standing on a huge one directly opposite the Faerie Queen. The lights swept around in an arc until they were focused on the two of them, and the music instantly dropped to a steady hum.

"You must stop this foolishness, my queen," boomed the Faerie King.

"Foolishness indeed," she responded archly.

"Your quarrel with me has upset the natural order of the world."

"It is *your* wanton behavior that has led us to this state, my *lord*."

"You are causing disorder and chaos all around us," he shouted as the music built and grew louder.

"*You* would be this furious if it were *I* who had been so faithless!" she howled, and they leaped into a dance that was sort of a chase through the rocks and around the hill.

As I watched, swaying, I suddenly felt two hands encircle my waist. Alex was clearly coming to his romantic senses at last. I leaned back into him happily.

"Can't get enough of me, huh, Hermia?" a voice bellowed in my ear.

Ok, NOT Alex. I leaped forward, spinning around.

Of all the places in all the world, what on EARTH was Pete Quincey doing HERE? He grinned and grabbed my hand.

"Come on, Hermia, we can have some fun, right? You, me, dark night, music . . . it's gotta be like, fate or something that we're both here tonight. Don't you want to dance?"

"Not with *you*," I said hotly.

"Admit it; I know you want me," he said, taking my other hand and trying to dance with me.

I paused for a moment, wondering if kicking in his

kneecaps would be a strong enough "no," and suddenly spotted Alex over Pete's shoulder.

Watching us.

Looking angry, or hurt, or both—it was hard to tell.

"Alex!" I called, wrenching my hands out of Pete's grip. "Wait!" I shoved Pete aside and ducked through the crowd of dancing people, toward the guy I was hopelessly in love with.

But he was gone.

Helena:

WELL. So this night wasn't going even *remotely* as planned.

Within moments of stepping through the gate, Dmitri had managed to lose us completely in the crowd. Or rather, lose *me*, I suppose. I turned around for a second and he was gone, leaving me with Pete and Nick. Oh, bliss.

We were far at the back of the crowd when we first came in, and I assure you I would have been happy to stay there, but Pete immediately started pushing his way forward, and as much as I loathed these guys, I didn't really want to be left alone in this madhouse.

The music was so loud I couldn't believe anyone could act in these conditions, especially with audience members everywhere dancing and screaming. I stumbled as we pressed forward and Nick turned back to me, leaning down to yell in my ear.

"Here, hold on to me," he shouted, and before I could protest, he'd clamped his giant paw around my hand and was dragging me along after him, *most* inelegantly, I might add. If I'd had a chance of being heard I would have questioned him as to who was really doing the holding here, but I had a feeling any attempt at conversation would be particularly useless.

All at once Pete shouted: "HEEYYYY!" and lunged away, abandoning me with Nick. We stopped and watched as a man (Aaron Rex, I assumed, although there were too many people between us for me to be sure) appeared in a flash of light and some sort of altercation took place on stage. I had no idea what was going on, or how this could in any way be considered interactive, for heaven's sake. It seemed like all the interacting involved was the audience jumping up and down madly to the music. I'll take nice, quiet, romantic Shakespeare any day, thank you very much.

We stood there awkwardly for a few minutes as music and people surged around us. This was not getting us, or more specifically me, anywhere. I could certainly not stand here with Nick all night, when I clearly had vital affairs of the heart to pursue, and possibly a best friend to rescue from whatever wreckage and chaos I had caused her. Not to mention that Nick was still holding on to my hand, and for some reason that was causing weird, butterfly-like flutterings in my stomach.

I tugged on Nick, and he leaned down again. Tall as I am, Nick was much taller, and I was hoping that would be helpful.

"Can you see Dmitri from up there? Or Hermia?" I shouted in his ear. (And can I mention how impossible it is to be graceful and shout at the same time?)

He stood up straight and surveyed the area. After a second, he leaned back down.

"No," he hollered. "But Alex is over under that big tree."

I looked where he was pointing and spotted Alex, just as he'd said. Alex wasn't looking nearly as happy as he should have . . . and where on earth was Hermia?

"I'm going to go check on him," I yelled.

"Ok," he said. "We'll meet outside the gate when it's over, ok?" I nodded and slipped away from him, edging my way slowly toward Alex.

As I got closer, I saw someone standing next to him and whispering in his ear. It was a small guy, or at least, I assumed it was a guy, with short spiky red hair and lines of rainbow glitter spiraling out from his face to trail down and around his all-black outfit. He handed Alex what looked like a note, nodded seriously, and melted back into the crowd.

Alex looked puzzled, but as he unfolded the note and read it, his expression changed to something more like surprise, and then resolve. I reached him just as he refolded it and looked up.

"Alex, hey," I said. "Where's Hermia?"

"Doesn't matter," he said, pocketing the note. "Want to dance?"

"Er," I said. "What? What happened to Hermia?"

"I'd rather be with you," he said intently.

"Okaayy, lunatic talk," I said. "That's very charming. Look, I'm sorry I brought Dmitri here—it's a long, terrible story involving a series of surprising and riveting coincidences—"

"Dmitri's here?" he said, surprised, and looked angry for a second. Then he shook his head firmly. "Forget about him," he said, taking my hand. "We've been invited to dance on stage." He started leading me through the crowd.

"Really?" I said. "I mean, what? Us? Me? Don't you mean Hermia?"

"No, you and me," he said. "Come on." He dived forward too quickly for me to argue, so I followed him, although I was most thoroughly bewildered by this strange turn of events. What was Alex going on about? Had he contracted the same crazy-boy syndrome that Dmitri was clearly suffering from? Or was he mocking me or something? And why wasn't he more surprised to see me here?

As we got closer to the rocks, suddenly the volume of the music surged (just when I'd thought it couldn't possibly get louder), and the lights swiveled to the man standing center stage. He threw up his hands, and the music stopped. Everyone froze.

"My queen will not see reason," he boomed slowly and deeply. A chord hummed, punctuating his statement. It was definitely Aaron Rex, the Faerie King—and although he was dressed very differently, I was almost certain that it was the same man who had let us in. He spread his arms toward the audience. "I will show her the folly of her ways. For this I need a mortal volunteer." *Thrumm,* the music went ominously.

Several of the "mortals" in the audience threw up their hands eagerly, mostly women, as far as I could tell. The Faerie King made a summoning gesture, and the small fellow I'd seen speaking to Alex earlier suddenly appeared next to the king, as if by magic.

"Robin, find me the mortal of my choice," Aaron Rex intoned, crossing his arms. Robin nodded, spun around three times, and leaped nimbly to the edge of a rock overhanging the audience. He surveyed the crowd, eyes half-closed, fingers pressed to his temples. All at once he pointed dramatically, and a spotlight obediently swiveled through the people leaping up and down for attention, spiraling around to focus on:

Nick Weaver.

Nick squinted and looked startled, even more so than the people near him who had actually tried to volunteer, while Nick clearly had not. He glanced around and stepped back, as if trying to get out of the light, but it followed him, implacable.

Onstage, Robin rose on his toes and beckoned imperiously.

There was a hushed pause as everyone stared at Nick, his head and shoulders rising monumentally out of the crowd. He glanced around again, confused, then shrugged and started forward. The audience parted before him in a sea of whispers and giggles.

The Faerie King nodded, looking smug, as Nick awkwardly climbed up the rocks to stand next to Robin. I noticed that Aaron Rex kept his distance from Nick, staying up a level as if he wanted to maintain the slight height advantage. He snapped his fingers at Robin, who instantly produced a cordless microphone from somewhere.

"Mortal," boomed the Faerie King. "I command you to sing for us."

Nick looked pale, but he gamely accepted the microphone. "No problem. Any preferences? 'The Star-Spangled Banner'?" he asked into it, his voice echoing around the enclosure.

"You are cocky, mortal," the king said menacingly. "I have chosen you as entertainment for my queen. Do you really think you're up for the challenge?"

Nick grinned. "Why not? I mean, I guess you're not doing so hot, right? Which is why you need to bring in a real man, like me." See that? He can act so confident and tough with everyone else, but when he gets around me there's stammering and destruction of foliage and fine art. It's simply mysterious.

Aaron Rex scowled and gestured offstage. The first few bars of a familiar song started up.

I saw Nick recognize it at the same time as I did: that old Frankie Lyman song from a million years ago, "Why Do Fools Fall in Love?" It was on one of my dad's old records that Nick and Hermia and I used to listen to in elementary school. At least it was a song he knew, if he could remember any of it. "Come on, Nick," I whispered. I found myself intently hoping that he could pull this off. He took a deep breath, lifted the microphone, and launched into the song.

Of course, there was the tiny problem that Nick was completely tone-deaf.

People around us winced as he belted out the words and shimmied across the stage. I guess some part of Nick figured, if you're going to look like an idiot, might as well look like a *total* idiot.

Well, mission accomplished. It was almost embarrassing enough to make me forgive him for the stuck-up snob comment—almost.

Hermia:

I couldn't believe it. Nick Weaver was here, too? Had *anyone* in our class gone to the junior prom? What were

Pete and Nick doing here? And how did he manage to get up on stage when *I* was clearly the perfect volunteer? Did he have some sort of radar for part stealing? *I* at least can sing, for pete's sake. It's one of my talents, not that Mr. Duke would know that, determined as he is to avoid musicals at all costs, the Renaissance-drama-obsessed buffoon. And if he did do a musical, he'd probably pick an Andrew Lloyd Webber, knowing HIS taste. Ye gods.

Not that this was the first thought on my mind at this point, of course. I couldn't find Alex anywhere—yet another tragic side effect of being so wretchedly short. Nick was up on stage, singing (if you want to call it that) as I battled my way through to the trees, when suddenly someone grabbed my wrist.

"Pete, I *said*—," I started, rounding on him, only to come face-to-face with DMITRI.

"*Dmitri?*" I yelped, shoving him forcefully away from me. Hadn't he ruined enough already? What was he doing here? HOW had he gotten in here? How did he even know—well, ok, *that* wasn't too hard to figure out. *For crying out loud, Helena*, I thought, *how is THIS plan supposed to win you back your truly beloved slimeball?*

"Alex has ditched you already, I see," he said with a reptilian smile. "You'd have been better off sticking with me."

"Have you seen Alex?" I said, suddenly worried. "You didn't do anything to him, did you?"

"What if I did?" he growled. "You're supposed to be with me tonight, remember?"

"I don't think there are enough words in the English language to express how much I loathe you," I snapped. "But hear this: If you did something to Alex, I swear I will personally pummel you upside the head until you rue the day you ever came to Athenwood. You'll rue the day you came anywhere near me. You'll rue the day you were BORN, sleazebag. You'll rue it A LOT." He actually looked startled by these threats. What, the other three million times I'd told him I hated him hadn't sunk in? I glared at him for a second, then turned and stomped away.

There was a lot that was much too weird about this situation, but I didn't have time to figure it out. I had to find Alex and warn him that Dmitri was here.

Up on stage, Nick was throwing himself into the song, belting out what lyrics he could remember. The music shifted into some sort of trumpet or saxophone solo.

"Dance, mortal!" the Faerie King boomed. I was starting to not like him very much. I mean, Nick is a goober, yes, but there was no need to make such an ass out of him in front of everybody.

"Stop this at once," another voice rang out through the sound system. The music cut off and Nick paused, squinting into the lights. Tanya Moon sailed regally out from beyond the hill, behind Aaron Rex. She went right past him and straight up to Nick. I realized there *was* music playing, but it was slowly and quietly building, and it was eerie-sounding, with a slow thumping rhythm.

"A mortal," she purred in a low, spine-chilling voice. *Thump thump*, went the music. "A mortal of my very own. How . . . thoughtful of you, my lord." *Thump thump*. Her hands wove around Nick, sliding over his shoulders, his arms. *Now* he looked really petrified.

"What?" the king barked.

"I love it," she said, reaching up to run her fingers through

Nick's hair. "I shall treasure it always." She smiled dangerously.

"Uh," Nick said nervously, his voice echoing through her cordless microphone as he twitched away from her. "Hang on."

"This fool is only meant to make you laugh, my lady," the king hissed. "He is a bauble, a plaything."

"I think there is more to him than that," she murmured, casting the king a sly look. "I choose to dance with him. Come, mortal," she said commandingly. "My faeries shall attend on you . . . and you shall be my *new* Faerie King."

"What?" the king roared thunderously, but an imperious wave of her hand brought the music up to a deafening level that drowned him out. The Faerie Queen's attendants leaped out and encircled her and Nick, sweeping them off to the far side of the hill. The lights swept away from the king and flew through the crowd, spinning and spotlighting everybody dancing. When they swooped back to the stage, the king was gone, and Robin was bringing people up to dance on the flat boulders at the lowest level of the hill.

And that's when I saw them.

Alex—and Helena. On stage. DANCING. With EACH OTHER.

What on *earth*?

Helena:

I experienced quite an unusual array of emotions as Nick Weaver was hauled off backstage by the glittering theatrical ensemble.

In the first place I was surprised, because the Faerie Queen, from what I had been able to figure out of the show so far, did not seem like the type to tolerate big oafish guys, let alone run her hands all over their shoulders and tell them they're wonderful.

Seeing her do that sparked another, stranger emotion, which took me a while to puzzle out. As bizarre as this sounds, I actually found myself wanting to run onstage and pull Nick away from her long sparkly nails and dark painted eyes. Now, I believe it is fairly clear to anyone who knows me that I am *not* the heroic rescuing type. That's really more Hermia's style. I'm the person to turn to for diplomacy and reasoning (neither of which are Hermia's forte), but when it comes to flinging oneself bodily in the way of disaster, it generally doesn't occur to me as a smart or elegant thing to do.

But for the first time ever, I had a very strong urge to do precisely that. I wanted to leap between them and tell her to stop messing with my friends, even my dopey gigantic haven't-spoken-to-them-in-years friends who think I'm a stuck-up snob. I wanted to tell Nick he had been very brave and only a little ridiculous. I wanted to help him escape from this vast, loud, confusing place where people like Dmitri and the Faerie King used our fragile emotions to mock us.

It was all very odd. I had to remind myself firmly that Nick Weaver is perfectly capable of taking care of himself, that he probably wouldn't appreciate me interfering, that it was only a play, and that I was already terribly busy trying to find my truly beloved, Dmitri. That was my priority here. The rest was just background noise.

Still, there was sort of a weird scrunching feeling in my stomach as Nick disappeared with the Faerie Queen. Completely and utterly inexplicable.

Then, of course, there was the shock I experienced when Alex abruptly seized my hand again and I found myself being launched onto the stage by him and that Robin guy.

"What are you *doing*?" I shrieked, batting them away.

"Dancing with the prettiest girl here," Alex said as Robin twirled off to haul up another couple.

"Alex, have you completely lost your mind?" I said. "What happened to Hermia? Why aren't you with her?"

"Would you stop going on about her?" he said. "I'm dancing with you instead, aren't I? Dmitri can have her, if he's dumb enough to want her instead of you."

"Ok, I may have pointed this out already," I said, "but *what*?"

"Helena!" A familiar voice sounded behind me. My heart leaped, although not as high or as hopefully as I thought it rightfully should have, all things considered.

"Dmitri?" I said, turning. He grabbed my arm, glaring at Alex.

"What are you doing with this guy?" he said to me.

"Back off, Gilbert," Alex barked.

"Me? Back off? *You're* the one messing with my girlfriend, pal." Dmitri put his other arm protectively around me, as I came perilously close to fainting with surprise.

"Your *girlfriend*?" I squeaked.

"Oh, bite me, Gilbert," Alex said at the same time.

"Helena, you know you're the only girl for me," Dmitri said soulfully. "'Shall I compare thee to a summer's day? Thou art—'"

"Shove it already, Dmitri; she knows you don't mean a word you say," Alex said, pushing him away from me and stepping between us. "You wanted Hermia, remember? Well, you can have her. She's in this crowd somewhere, and she's completely available. I, on the other hand, will be sticking with Helena, who is the only girl for *me*, so get lost."

"Oh my GOD," I said, understanding hitting me like an enormous truck. There was only one explanation for this. "I get it. I see what you're doing. You guys are making fun of me! You are deliberately *torturing* me for your own amusement! You think this is some sort of game, don't you? Do you think it's hilarious and . . . and *cool* to kid around with a person's *feelings* like this?"

"I'm not kidding around, Helena," Alex said, looking a little confused.

"Me neither," Dmitri chimed in. "Helena, I was wrong to ever want Hermia. My heart has seen the light, and it is you." He gave Alex a furious look, but I knew better. I was convinced I could detect a glimmer of glee in there.

"Yeah, right," said Alex. "Like anybody would fall for a line like that."

"You don't know anything about true love," Dmitri said. "Don't mock what you don't understand."

"*I'm* the only one getting mocked here!" I cried. The music was giving me the worst kind of headache, and every so often one of the other dancing couples on the nearby rocks would smack into us and nearly knock me over. AND YET, I'll have you know, NEITHER of these boys who were supposedly suddenly all into me seemed even *remotely* inclined to leap to my rescue and defend my personal space. Noooooooo. They were too busy puffing up their chests and talking rubbish.

Suddenly, like a beacon in a storm, I saw a friendly face appear before me. Hermia fought her way through the crowd and scrambled up onstage. And she didn't even look mad to see me (and Dmitri) there, or at least, not too mad. Mostly just puzzled, actually.

"There you are!" she said breathlessly to Alex. "Thank God—I thought I'd lost you! I was having terrible visions of never finding you again and wasting away in despair and possibly having to walk home over the George Washington Bridge, or worse yet call my dad." She smiled, but he didn't smile back.

"You looked like you were having enough fun without me," he said. "So I'm dancing with Helena now."

"With—with Helena?" Hermia gave me a *What the? Are all boys this crazy?* look.

"Yeah," Alex said, taking my hand. "In fact, I'm thinking of asking her out."

"You're *what*?" Hermia and I shrieked simultaneously.

"I don't believe this!" she said.

Something was really strange here. Why would the boys be acting like this? Where had any of this weird behavior come from? Then in a flicker of the lights I was suddenly sure I saw Hermia wink at Alex, and all my worst fears came crashing in on me.

"Yeah, neither do I," I said, pulling my hand free and stepping away from all of them. "I don't believe *any* of this. There's no way Alex would do this without you telling him to, Hermia. And I guess you put Dmitri up to it, too?"

"What are you talking about?" she said.

"Whose idea was it?" I said, my voice rising. "Did you come up with this tonight, here? Or have you been planning this all along? Is this some sort of twisted joke? Do all our years of friendship mean nothing to you?"

"I don't think *I'm* the one being twisted here," Hermia said. "*You're* the one who's acting all crazy!"

"Oh, there is no nobility in the world, none," I cried in outrage. "There is no loyalty, no true friendship, nothing at all that one can count on. Certainly not love, and apparently not even your best friend. The world is just one GIANT BLACK HOLE of misery and loneliness, and I, I who thought I had everything a girl could want in life but three weeks ago, I am now *forlorn* and *abandoned*. And *woeful*." I buried my face in my hands.

"Oh my God, melodramatic much?" Hermia snapped. "Isn't 'forlorn' and 'woeful' just the way you like it, Miss *I'm*-a-real-poet-I-know-*all*-about-suffering-no-one-*understands*-the-depths-of-my-desolation-and-agony-especially-not-my-shallow-friend-Hermia blah blah blah?"

"That is not what I mean," I said, lifting my head and flinging my hair back. "*This* is not in the LEAST BIT romantic. Or poetic. There is *nothing* beautiful about being tormented by your supposed friends, I *don't* feel magical or wistful or anything like that, and this music is driving me completely *insane*. I want to go HOME."

"Well, no one asked you to come here in the first place!" she yelled.

"Is that what this is about?" I shouted back. "Is this some elaborate scheme to get back at me for telling Dmitri where you went? I'm *sorry*, ok? I hardly think making your hordes of admirers pretend to like me is the most mature response!"

"She didn't make me do anything," Alex suddenly interjected.

"Me neither," Dmitri agreed quickly.

"I decided I want to be with someone who knows how

to seriously care about a person," Alex said, taking my hand, but watching Hermia.

"Me too," Dmitri said, taking my other hand, his eyes on Alex.

"Do you have any original thoughts *ever*?" Hermia said to Dmitri. She looked at Alex as if she'd just been stabbed in the heart. Lord almighty, I knew she was a good actress, but I had no idea she could concoct a complicated revenge scenario like this. *And the Oscar goes to . . .*

"You want to take this outside, little man?" Alex said threateningly to Dmitri. I considered pointing out that we *were* outside, but decided that was unnecessary, as this was clearly all an act anyway.

"Absolutely," Dmitri shouted. "I'll take you *down*, Sanders!" They both let go of my hands and started for the edge of the stage.

"Wait!" Hermia cried, catching hold of Alex's hand. "Alex, are you completely high? Why are you being like this?"

"Go on, keep up the charade," I said. "It only gets funnier and funnier, doesn't it? The more my heart breaks? Ha-ha-ha! Laugh at the poor woebegone loveless girl! Her misery is so amusing!"

"Let me go, Hermia," Alex said forcefully.

"Are you going to let a girl keep you from fighting me?" Dmitri taunted.

"Not a chance," Alex said, shaking himself free. "Come on, Gilbert, let's see if you're still the hair-puller you were in seventh grade." They both jumped off the stage and vanished into the dancing mob of audience members, all of whom seemed singularly oblivious to us.

I pressed my fingertips under my eyes, trying not to cry. I could picture them getting out of sight and stopping to roar with laughter at the clever, clever scene they had just played.

"You!" Hermia whirled on me, her eyes flashing. "This is all *your* fault, isn't it, you sneaking, theatrical, backstabbing—"

"*Me* backstabbing?" I yelped. "*You're* the one who stole Dmitri first, remember? And now I've seen this little game of yours, it is all too abundantly clear that nothing is too low for you."

"Low?" she yelled, raising her voice as the music got, unbelievably, even louder than it was before. "Is *that* how you did it? By pointing out how short I am? Did you use your tall I'm-so-gorgeous supermodel looks to seduce him away from me, is that it?"

"Sure, just pile on the derision, there, little miss," I said. "As *if* my looks could have that kind of effect!"

"Well, what else could it be? Guys don't just randomly fall for girls while they're on practically-almost-semi-dates with other girls, do they?"

"Not unless *someone* tells them to, I imagine!"

"You think that great beanpole height of yours is some kind of protection?" Hermia said angrily, stepping toward me. "You think because I'm so much shorter than you I can't take you in a fight or something?"

"I'm not going to fight you, Hermia," I said in alarm. I've *seen* the way she fights, or at least, I remember it from elementary school, when she took down most of the boys in our class during recess for making fun of my poetry.

"What are you, scared?" she said.

"Um, *yeah*," I said. "I am a *poet*. I don't *fight* people."

"You got a better idea?"

"I certainly do," I said, leaped off the stage, and ran.

ACT V

June 6

Hermia:

I stood paralyzed onstage for a minute in utter bewilderment as Helena pelted off into the crowd.

Why was she being so crazy? Why was Alex being so . . . weird?

What in the name of Pete was going on?

Oh.

Oh, man, *Pete* . . .

My heart sank. I had completely forgotten about him in the chaos of finding Dmitri and Helena here. Was that why Alex was acting all crazy? But why would he turn to Helena . . . why would he think she would even be interested in him? What made him think she was "someone who knows how to seriously care about a person"? *I* care! I *so* care. I care *very* seriously! How on earth had he missed all the seriously caring about him I'd been doing? I'd been all *about* "seriously caring" about him for like *months* now!

I climbed off the stage and pushed my way into the crowd. I wasn't even sure what was going on in the show anymore. I had the vague impression that there had been faerie-types dancing around singing about something, but I couldn't really concentrate on it. It was silly of me anyway to think I could get talent-spotted in a situation like this. Also, I could pursue my career anytime, but this might be the last chance I had to get Alex to ask me out.

At least I didn't think the boys had actually gotten to a place where they could fight. I had seen that Robin guy watching us argue, and he took off after them when they jumped off the stage. The theater company probably didn't want people brawling in the immediate area—bad for business and all that.

I wriggled through the crowd until I found myself near the concrete structure, far in the back corner, among the trees. A silvery door loomed in front of me, labeled HEROINES. I pushed my way inside and yes, luckily, it was a ladies' room, complete with a couch and everything.

I checked under the doors first, but there was only one pair of shoes visible, and they definitely weren't Helena's—far too huge and sparkly. With a sigh I took some paper towels and started washing my face.

"I'm not going to cry, I'm not going to cry," I told myself, splashing cold water over my wrists. I heard the toilet flush behind me as I lifted a wet paper towel and pressed it to my face.

"Cry about what?" a low, husky voice said. I dropped the paper towel and spun around.

"Tanya Moon!" I gasped.

"Oops. You caught me," she said with a sly grin.

She was more than tall. She was lofty. She was *statuesque*. (Although the four-inch platform heels were definitely an unfair advantage.) She seemed to be covered in glitter from head to toe, and she was wearing a floor-length cape that shimmered like dragonfly wings. Her hair was midnight black and piled on her head, with golden threads woven through it. She lifted one gold-covered eyebrow at me.

"Do you want to talk about it?" she said.

"But—" I stammered. "Don't you have to be out there? Aren't you supposed to be performing?"

She shrugged. "I'm taking a break. Aaron gets to have his fabulous ranting scene next. So if you don't mind missing that, we can chat for a minute ... I like to make him worry about where I am." She smiled slyly again. "This night isn't going *quite* the way he expected, either."

"Really?" I said. "I thought he pretty much controlled the whole thing."

"He likes to think so." She stretched languorously and sank down on the red couch, like a great cat. "But there are ways upon ways to meddle with his plans." In fact, her smile made her look like a cat who'd eaten several small birds. I felt a twinge of concern as I remembered poor Nick being carted away.

"Anyway," Tanya went on. "He's being a little more arrogant than I like tonight. So take your time. Tell me your story." She fastened her eyes on mine. "Be *fascinating*."

I hopped up to sit on the counter, and before I knew it, the whole story was pouring out of me. Helena and her misguided passion for pompous, self-important Dmitri. My dad forbidding me to come, and our stealth plan to get here anyway. Stupid Pete Quincey and his unexpected mucking-everything-up. And Alex Alex Alex, the guy I'd been adoring for *months* and who, as far as I could tell, was as far away from getting my hints and declaring his undying love as he'd ever been.

"Can you blame me for being totally confused and a little upset?" I said. "I mean, here I am, stranded in Central Park. Alex has finally decided to ask someone out, except it's NOT ME. My so-called 'devoted admirer' Dmitri, who caused all this stupidity in the first place, *also* doesn't want to date me anymore, proving his idiotic boyness once again, *not* that I would ever have him anyway. Not to mention my best friend Helena has somehow stolen both of their hearts and for some TOTALLY UNFATHOMABLE reason is mad at *me*. At me! What did I ever do to her? Plus I think my dad is going to *kill* me. I might not even be exaggerating there. I maybe should never go home, just in case. Not that I have any way of getting there anyway, if Alex is really mad at me, but I don't get why he would be. I mean, I'm obviously crazy about him, aren't I? If he liked me too, wouldn't he have done something about it by now? Why would he be acting like this about Helena?

"ARRRRRRRRRRRRRRRRRRRRRRRRRRRRRRRGH." I looked at Tanya Moon, who was still staring at me intently.

"What do *you* think?" I said.

"Me?" she said languidly. "I don't dispense advice, my dear. In any case, you don't need it. The answers are right in front of you."

"They are?" I said.

"This Alex boy," she said. "He knows you like him, right?"

"I should think so," I said. "I mean, I'm like the least subtle person in history."

"So you've told him you like him," she said, leaning back into the couch.

"Well . . . not in so many words. But I hang out with him all the time, and, and I smile at him a lot, and I haven't dated anyone else in like MONTHS, and plus, hey, I keep dropping all these hints."

"Ah, yes, you mentioned the hints," she said. "And most guys are quite skillful at picking up on these 'hints,' are they?"

"Um," I said. "Actually . . ."

"Because this behavior of yours is quite different, is it, from the way you used to act before you wanted to date him? And quite different from the way you act around anyone else?"

"Er," I said. "Well . . ."

"So since you have been as clear as it is possible to be, it's entirely inconceivable that he could be in the least bit confused about your true feelings."

"Huh," I said. "When you put it that way . . ."

"Moving on," she said. "The situation tonight. I should tell you that I would not be at all surprised if my dear meddling co-star had something to do with it."

"Aaron Rex?" I said. "Wait, how? Why would he be involved?"

She sighed expressively.

"I don't suppose," she said, "that your friends might have been the last audience members to arrive, might they?"

"I don't know," I said, puzzled. "Maybe—they probably left quite a bit later than us."

"Aaron likes to"—she paused, pursing her lips—"let's say, play these little *games* with the audience, particularly the last people to arrive. He hates people who are late to the theater. He thinks it means they don't take us seriously. That poor boy he pulled out of the audience to sing? Just one of his innocent victims." She rolled on before I had a chance to ask what had happened to Nick. "He uses his little emissary, Robin, to deliver messages between people . . . messages they didn't actually send. If there's any way he could have confused your Alex with this Dmitri, it's possible Alex received a message allegedly from Helena that wasn't actually intended for him."

"The Athenwood sweatshirts!" I cried, jumping off the counter. "They were both wearing them!"

"There you go," she purred, uncoiling herself from the couch. "Now, I should get back to the show. But I will tell you one thing, as cliché as it may sound. Don't lose your friend Helena over this. Very few men are worth it." She strolled over to the mirror, pressing her long manicured hands delicately to her hair.

"You know who might be, though," she mused, watching herself. "That lovely boy I rescued from Aaron's clutches." She smiled, baring her teeth. "According to Aaron's script for tonight, the Faerie Queen was supposed to be 'equally amused' by the 'foolish spectacle,' and mocking the fellow was supposed to 'bring us together.' But I felt sorry for him, didn't you? There is a real heart in that boy. When I got him backstage, I offered him the chance to come back out at the end and dance with me . . . a kind of redemption, to offset his earlier humiliation, you might say. And can you imagine? He refused!" She turned to give me a wide-eyed look.

"He said there's a girl here whom he cares about very much, and even if she never returns his affection, he doesn't want her to think he might ever be interested in someone else—not even a famous actress such as myself." Tanya Moon laughed delightedly. "And then he insisted he had to go find her and make sure she was all right, because she was having a rough night. Isn't that the most delectable thing? I do so adore stories of unrequited love."

"Hmmm," I said. "I think I prefer my love requited, actually." We smiled at each other in the mirror. "Thanks very much, Ms. Moon," I said. "You were really helpful."

"Well, for goodness sakes, don't tell anyone," she said. "I'm supposed to be terribly aloof and unapproachable, don't you know."

"Yes, ma'am." I grinned. "Your secret's safe with me."

"And I think when the time comes to tell this Alex how you really feel," she said, pausing with her hand on the door handle, "you'll know." She whisked out the door, leaving me alone in the bathroom.

I glanced at myself in the mirror and hurriedly tried to reorganize my hair into something presentable.

Tanya Moon was right. If I wanted Alex to know how I felt about him, I would have to tell him myself.

But first I had to find him.

Helena:

My legs were sore from being braced against the stall door and my face was bright pink with the effort of breathing quietly by the time Hermia finally scooted out the door behind Tanya Moon.

I let my breath out with a whoosh, stood up stiffly, and peered out into the room.

Empty. They were gone.

And I was completely, utterly, thoroughly befuddled.

Not about what had happened, so much. It all made a weird kind of sense now—I had even seen Robin give Alex a note, whatever it said. And Hermia hadn't known a thing about it. I should have realized that, but one could hardly expect me to properly concentrate in all the din out there, could one? Perhaps it had been my guilty conscience driving me to insane defensive conclusions.

But mostly I found myself thinking about Nick. Tall, bumbling, goofy Nick Weaver, who couldn't sing to save his life, but who maybe, just maybe, didn't hate me so much after all.

What other girl could he have meant when he said that to Tanya Moon, right?

Was it possible he still liked me?

Why did that thought make me so bizarrely . . . happy?

I knew one thing. I was sick of feeling pathetic and worthless. I was sick of being the mopey, neglected, obsessive friend that everyone laughs at. In fact, I thought, I am quite fed up with destiny altogether. Was it my destiny to lose my best friend and my soul mate at a show in the middle of Central Park and discover I have a completely empty life at the age of seventeen? I THINK NOT. I think perhaps I've been trying too hard to help destiny out. I think from now on destiny can JOLLY WELL COME FIND ME.

And you know what—I didn't need Dmitri to be part of it. That's it. Someone ELSE could be his blasted soul mate, because this, quite frankly, was not the romantic story I wanted to be telling my grandchildren anyway.

I straightened my dress and smoothed out my hair.

All right then. Let's go sort things out.

Hermia:

I emerged into a confusion of noise and flashing lights. The Faerie King's attendants were on stage, arguing with the Faerie Queen's attendants, which evidently required a lot of singing and dancing and leaping and howling. It was very *West Side Story*, only with more glitter and no knives.

I could do that! I thought, watching them. *I'd be a great faerie attendant!* Maybe I could use my new connection with Tanya Moon to blackmail her into putting me in the show. Hee hee hee.

But first things first: finding Alex.

I circled through the crowd, struck with an unsurprising sense of déjà vu. *Ok, Alex*, I thought, *this is the very last date*

I'm going to spend getting stomped on by vast hordes of tall people while trying to find you. A girl has got to have some standards.

I recognized the joking-with-myself as my typical reaction to being nervous, and hoped that it wouldn't translate into saying something chipper and idiotic, the way it usually did.

There was no sign of Alex anywhere. He couldn't really have left, could he?

I was starting to get seriously concerned about ever finding him when there was a sudden burst of light and sound onstage. Everyone in the audience stopped dancing to watch as the Faerie King and Queen leaped out from behind the hill and faced each other, sweeping their attendants aside. I made a small effort to keep sidling and peering around, but people in the crowd kept giving me funny looks, so I had to content myself with standing still on tiptoe, scanning the dark sea of faces.

"My lady," rumbled Aaron Rex.

"My *lord*," she replied, half-mockingly.

"Where is the mortal plaything?" he boomed.

"I released him," she said sweetly. "His inner nobility was too charming to keep caged, so I set him free."

The king's eyes narrowed. "I thought you had chosen him as my replacement."

"Do you feel your position so easily threatened, sir?" she said, dancing toward him. "Do you think perhaps in future you might not . . . treat it so lightly?"

"Perhaps," he said. "Love is a serious business, is it not, my queen?"

"It is," she said. "It can make people do the most ridiculous things. But we should celebrate our love by bringing others together. Don't you agree?"

"Certainly," the king boomed. Tanya Moon snapped her fingers twice in the air. Two of her attendants darted off and reappeared with Robin and someone else.

Someone in corduroys and an Athenwood sweatshirt.

I gasped as Alex lifted his hand to block the lights from his eyes. He seemed aghast to find himself onstage.

"I believe someone here has something to say to this young man," the Faerie Queen declared, smiling sinisterly at the audience.

What, here? Now? In front of all these people? I could feel myself turning pink. *See if I ever spill my guts to a drama queen in a ladies' room again.*

"And what better way to say it . . . than to sing it?" the king agreed, looking equally menacing. The pulsating music receded and slowly a new song came drifting over the speakers.

I started laughing. Ok, this was underhanded and crazy, but at least she had chosen her torture device wisely. Not only did I know it, and it said everything perfectly, but it was in my range, too! *Ok, Hermia,* I thought. *This is your moment. Seize the, you know, carp, or whatever it is.*

I started working my way forward, and I wasn't surprised when a spotlight found me and the crowd parted. Robin met me at the foot of the stage and handed me a microphone.

*". . . they keep saying
We laugh just a little too loud. . . ."*

I felt like I looked about twice as silly as Nick Weaver had, but what could I do? I had wanted to volunteer, hadn't

I? A jolt like electricity ran through me as I realized what was happening.

I was ONSTAGE. ME! Singing! Performing! In front of hundreds of people! Plus Aaron Rex and Tanya Moon! In the front rows I could see faces smiling. That's right, audience! Look out! A star is born!

It was the most amazing feeling. I decided right then that Dad would never be able to stop me, juvenile delinquent school or not. I was right all along. This was definitely my destiny.

I focused now on Alex, letting the audience melt away behind me. At first he looked suspicious, but gradually his expression started to change. I belted on—just me and Bonnie Raitt.

"Let's give them something to talk about
How about love, love, love, love?"

As the second chorus came on, another voice joined mine. I turned around to find Tanya Moon singing along. She winked at me and turned to the audience, encouraging them to join in, which they did (thank goodness, because it was starting to get a little overwhelming!). Faeries crowded to the front of the stage, leaving Alex and me standing far in the back, on a level rock off to the side.

We looked at each other shyly.

"Soooo," I said.

"Wow," he said. "That was phenomenal."

"You might have known I'd get you up here one way or another, right?" I joked.

"Yeah, what—what was that all about? The, uh . . . song thing."

"I made the mistake of over-sharing with a faerie queen," I said wryly. He looked down at his shoes.

"So that was . . . it didn't mean—"

"Oh, no, it *did* mean," I said quickly. "I mean, it *totally* meant. It was *full* of meaning. And seriousness. And serious caring. If that's ok. I guess it could *not* mean, if you didn't want it to mean—"

"I want it to mean," he said, taking my hands. I looked up into his eyes and felt another electric-like shock thrill through me. He smiled. I smiled.

"So, you wouldn't rather be dating Helena?" I asked.

"Well, *apparently* this note I got earlier wasn't from her after all. Or meant for me, for that matter. That's what they tell me backstage. I guess I'll have to make do with you instead." He winked.

"Do I get to see this spellbinding note?" I said. "I'm very curious about what a girl could say to magically transform a guy like that."

He fished it out and handed it to me, looking a little abashed.

Hey there,
Sick of unrequited love?
Me too.
Give me a chance—let's dance.
Helena

"Wow," I said.

"I know," he said.

"You're kind of like a moron," I said (nicely).

"Yeah," he agreed.

"I mean, this is clearly not her handwriting. It doesn't look like any girl's handwriting, let alone the ever-perfect, always-elegant, absolutely-flowery Miss Helena. And in the second place, there are WAY too many one-syllable words in this note. Did you really think she wrote this?"

"Well," he said. "It wasn't *completely* impossible. Plus it's pretty dark out here, didn't you notice?"

"I'm sticking with the 'you're kind of like a moron' theory," I said. "So this is all a girl has to say to get you to ask her out?"

"I guess she'd really have to be the right girl," he said, putting away the note and taking my hands again with a smile. "Sooo . . . *you* wouldn't rather be dating Pete Quincey?"

"YUCK," I said. "Alex, believe me. There is no one I am *less* interested in dating. Except Dmitri, of course. And there's only one person I *am* interested in dating. Ok?"

"Ah," he said. "Nick Weaver, huh?"

I smacked him on the arm. "Actually," I said, "I'm hoping I can get a certain someone *else* interested in him after what I heard tonight."

"Really?" he said curiously.

"Yup," I said. "I'll tell you the whole story later. But there's something vitally important I have to do first."

"What's that?" he said.

"Somehow trick you into kissing me," I said, tilting my head at him. "Because it would be *highly* inappropriate for me to kiss you first, you know. Helena would be very firm on how unladylike that would be."

"You, ladylike?" he teased. "In what alternate dimension, exactly?"

"Hey," I said. "I was very ladylike about waiting for you to figure out you liked me, wasn't I? I sent lots of demure hints and politely allowed you *eons* of time to make the first move."

"*Oh*," he said. "Is *that* what was going on?"

"Of course!" I said. "Were you waiting for me to ask *you* out? Didn't you get my hints? They were VERY CLEAR hints."

"They were?" he said. "There were hints? What hints?"

"Oh, *boys*," I said, rolling my eyes.

He pulled me toward him. "Sorry I was dense," he said.

"I think being dragged onstage and sung to in front of hundreds of people is probably punishment enough," I said, wrapping my arms around his neck.

"Um, yeah," he said. "Let's never do that again."

And then (FIIIIIIIIIIIIIIIIIIIIIIIIIIIIIIIINALLY) ...he kissed me!

Helena:

Well, Hermia had certainly taken Tanya Moon's words to heart. I was thanking my lucky stars I hadn't revealed my presence in there. *Imagine* if the Faerie Queen had made *me* sing! In front of all those people! To a boy! Can you picture anything less refined? My mother would have been thoroughly shocked, I would think.

But if anyone could pull it off, it was Hermia. I don't know if she could tell, in the midst of the singing, but the way Alex was looking at her was too sweet for words.

So those two might work it out after all, I thought. *Now I just need to find—*

"Helena?"

I was smiling already as I turned around.

"Nicholas," I said, flipping back my hair. He loomed over

me, all six foot four of him, as goofy and awkward and surprisingly studly as ever. He paused and regarded me curiously, a half-smile playing across his face.

"You haven't called me that since—"

"Since eighth grade," I finished.

"*Nobody* calls me that anymore," he said. He looked suddenly more relaxed than I'd seen him be in my presence in years. It was as if a mountain of tension were melting out of him. Hmmmm. I'd have to think of a more romantic way to phrase that, once it came time to write poems about this.

"Right, sorry," I said. "Which is it your illustrious companions prefer? Dude or jackass?"

"Nicholas is fine with me," he said, grinning.

"You were quite a superstar up there, Nicholas," I said. "I was fair tempted to rescue you."

"Wish you had," he said. "But I survived! I had to fight my way out. It took some serious manliness. Lucky I'm all tough and stuff. There were monsters back there, Helena! Ok, people wielding glitter. Glitter! Try to imagine me in glitter. Then imagine old Pete seeing me in glitter."

"Then proceed directly to you being tormented about glitter for the rest of your life," I finished.

"Pretty much," he said.

"A sparkly football player," I mused. "It sounds positively riveting. I'll make sure to talk to Ms. Mason about working it into the costume design."

"Don't you dare," he said.

"You'll have to get past my bodyguard if you want to stop me," I said. "And you *know* Hermia can totally take you."

"Hmmm," he said. "True."

"Nick . . . can I ask you a question?"

"Sure." He looked apprehensive.

"All right." I steeled myself. This was the moment of truth. "Is it true—" I couldn't meet his eyes. There was no hope of approaching this elegantly. "Nicholas . . . is it true that you think I'm a stuck-up snob?"

"What?" I felt his hands on my shoulders and looked up to see that he was studying my face intently. "Why would you think that?"

"Well, Chrissy Canton said—"

"Chrissy Canton!" he exclaimed. "You mean the Chrissy Canton whose dream in life is to be a gossip columnist?"

"Well . . . yes," I said, turning pink. "Are you saying she invented the whole thing?"

"I certainly don't remember saying anything like that," he said with a puzzled expression.

"Really?" I said.

"Oh," he said suddenly. "Oh, wait."

"Oh, WAIT?" I said. "You mean you *did* say it? And you *forgot* about it?"

"No, no," he said hurriedly, catching my hand as I started to pull away. "She misrepresented the situation."

"Oh, I *see*," I said imperiously. "You meant 'stuck-up snob' in the *nice* way." (I did allow him to keep holding my hand, though. Just until he explained himself, I figured. It would only be polite.) (And not stuck-up!)

"I did!" he protested. "Or, I mean, that's not what I meant."

"Nicholas, you're not making any sense."

"This was ages ago—ninth grade, I think. Back when Chrissy was trying to get a gossip column added to the school paper. She told me she was doing this poll about perceptions of people. And one of the questions she asked me was whether I thought you were (a) a stuck-up snob or (b) a heartless intellectual elitist."

"You can't possibly be serious," I said, astounded.

"I said neither, of course," he rushed on. "But she insisted that I pick an answer to every question. So I made her promise she wouldn't print anything I'd said. I never thought she'd turn around and flat out *tell* you."

"Why would she do that?" I asked.

"I dunno," he said, scratching his head. "She was following me around a lot for most of freshman year, actually."

"Do you think she was hoping you'd ask her out?" I said, light suddenly dawning. That would certainly explain a few things.

"Me?" he said, astonished. "I doubt it."

"Nonsense, Nicholas," I said. "You're really quite a catch. Didn't you know?" I smiled up at him.

"I am?" he said.

"Sure," I said. "You're sweet, and smart, and rather handsome, with a surprisingly adept grasp of Shakespeare. Not to mention your charming penchant for accidental destruction of inanimate objects."

He grinned sheepishly and looked thoughtful for a second.

"So, uh, Helena," he said. "In that case—can I ask—"

"Yes?" I said encouragingly.

"Uh," he said. "That is . . ."

"That is?" I prompted.

"See," he said. "Um. What I mean to say is, um." He shuffled his feet a bit. If I remembered correctly, it had gone much like this in eighth grade, too. But strangely, I was finding it much cuter now.

At that (dreadfully inopportune) moment, I spotted Dmitri working his way through the crowd toward us, bright red and looking seriously disheveled.

"Helena!" he cried. "There you are!" He looked Nick up and down disdainfully, and I suddenly noticed how short Dmitri looked next to Nick. Was he shorter than me? How would I not have noticed that before?

"I've had the most horrific experience," Dmitri went on. "This strange little person wouldn't let Sanders and me leave the show. He dragged us backstage and practically forced us to tell him what was going on. Then that queen creature came in, asked us our names, and SENT ME AWAY. Can you imagine the nerve? As if Sanders could possibly be more suited to being onstage than I am! Then there was more singing and noise and it's all quite unbearable." He glanced at Nick again. "Helena, can I speak to you in private for a moment?"

"Well . . . ," I said, a little torn. There had to be a reason I'd fallen for Dmitri in the first place, wasn't there? Shouldn't I give him a chance to explain himself?

"Come on," Dmitri said, taking my hand and tugging me away. I gave Nick a look that I sincerely hoped said *wait right there* and followed Dmitri into a corner by the fence.

"Helena," he began, clasping my hand and staring into my eyes. "I've been a fool."

"I'LL say," I said agreeably.

He paused, looking momentarily offended, then wrestled his expression back to contrition. "I don't know what I was thinking. Hermia is so clearly wrong for me. I mean, did you see her singing a little while ago? I could never date someone who would make such a spectacle of themselves in public. Whereas you are quiet and graceful and feminine in every way, and I see now that we are quite simply perfect for each other. I know I'm your soul mate,

Helena. And I'm prepared now to take you back."

"Hmmmmm," I said, gently extracting my hands from his grip. "That *is* a lovely offer, Dmitri. But as it happens, I've found somebody else. Sorry." I patted him reassuringly on the shoulder, managed not to laugh at his thunderstruck expression, turned around, and walked away.

Soul mate! shrieked a tiny corner of my mind. *Enduring! Committed! Working through obstacles! True love!*

Oh, shut up, the rest of my brain argued back, and rather convincingly, too, I might add.

Nick was standing where I'd left him, leaning against a tree and watching the play (which was really now a procession of sparkly people dancing) nervously, as if he expected the attendants to leap off the stage and assault him with glitter at any moment. The bright colored lights had swept around to the center of the area, leaving us in shadows on the outskirts. The only illumination here came from the moon, shining through the trees, surrounding us with a silvery glow.

"Nicholas." I touched his arm and he turned toward me, his eyes widening. I smiled, and slowly the sweetest grin spread across his face. I took his hand in mine and said:

"Is this what you were trying to say?"

And I leaned forward—and kissed him.

EPILOGUE

Sunday, June 8,
& Beyond

Poetess: Psst! Hermia! Are you on? Are you allowed to IM?

AmazonGrrrl!: I'm here! But we're treading carefully with my dad right now, so like, type quietly. ;)

Poetess: Are you still alive? Has your dad decided to disown you completely yet?

AmazonGrrrl!: After he promised Mr. Duke not to be too hard on me? He knows perfectly well I'm the biggest tattletale, and Dad likes to keep up good relations with our lovely, wonderful, brilliant director. Almost makes you wonder if there's some blackmail going on there . . .

Poetess: I tell you, Hermia, I nearly went into cardiac arrest when we drove back into the high school parking lot and your DAD was sitting RIGHT THERE on the steps.

AmazonGrrrl!: I know! You think YOU were scared! Here's me and Alex and you and Nick in a car, my prom dress stashed in the back, with Dmitri nowhere in sight (by the way, yay for Pete agreeing to drive him home in Nick's car, since none of US wanted to spend any time trapped in a small space with him). I was sure Dad was going to have an instant conniption.

Poetess: I was convinced he'd throw you on a plane and pack you off to Maine immediately!

AmazonGrrrl!: I still don't get why Polly and Mr. Duke were there, but thank heaven they were.

Poetess: I think Ms. Mason was pleasantly surprised at what a nice time she had at dinner with Theo. And she somehow pieced together that there might be something fishy going on with you and me and the junior prom. So she convinced him to come back to the high school and wait for the returning buses with her.

AmazonGrrrl!: And I guess Dad got suspicious, because he always does, and decided not to wait for Dmitri to drop me off, the way I said he would.

Poetess: I think Ms. Mason and Theo managed to calm him down a lot.

AmazonGrrrl!: Oh, yes. We definitely managed to scale down from bellowing to shouting, which was a *substantial* improvement.

Poetess: And you're only grounded for the rest of the school year.

AmazonGrrrl!: Apart from the time I'm needed in the theater, of course.

Poetess: Where *luckily* a certain carpenter/electrician just *happens* to spend most of his time . . . ;)

AmazonGrrrl!: And hey! No all-girls' penitentiary school in Maine next year!

Poetess: I liked Theo's point about who you would end up dating in an all-female environment. That certainly got your dad's attention. Theo can be pretty convincing when it comes to clinging to his already-fairly-meager stage crew.

AmazonGrrrl!: *Meager*? What are you implying, missy?

Poetess: Has anyone ever told you that you have a tiny complex about your height?

AmazonGrrrl!: TINY?!

Poetess: This is definitely my cue to sidle away nonchalantly. ;) And actually, I have to meet with Nicholas to run lines. Only four days until opening night! Oh my goodness!

AmazonGrrrl!: Tell me about it! The light cues are SO not ready!

Poetess: Well, I imagine it *might* impede the progress of the light cues when the Master Electrician and the Light Board Operator can't stop laughing about how much they looooooooooove each other.

AmazonGrrrl!: Oh, RIGHT, and I'm sooooooo sure you guys will be doing lots of useful "memorizing." Maybe in between all the SMOOOOCHING.

Poetess: *hee hee*

Poetess: I mean, stop that.

AmazonGrrrl!: Ok, ok.

Poetess: Don't forget that I'm cooking you dinner next weekend.

AmazonGrrrl!: And remind me why that was?

Poetess: You want me to say it AGAIN?

AmazonGrrrl!: YUP.

Poetess: *deeply aggrieved sigh* ;) All right, all right: to say I'm sorry for, you know, telling Dmitri where you were and then getting all mad at you for something you would clearly never in a million years even begin to remotely conceive of ever doing.

AmazonGrrrl!: Thaaaat's right.

Poetess: You know this is going to come back to haunt you the following weekend, when *you* cook *me* dinner to apologize for calling me backstabbing and melodramatic.

AmazonGrrrl!: And also for nearly jumping on you and tearing out all your hair. ☺

Poetess: Hey, trying to repress over here!

AmazonGrrrl!: Well, I figure I'll milk my turn at the head of the apology table while I can. ☺ It's only fair.

Poetess: I think you're my favorite person in the whole wide world.

AmazonGrrrl!: I think you're my favorite person in the whole wide universe.

Poetess: Really? Even more than "perfect splendid wonderful" Alex?

AmazonGrrrl!: Well, sure. Like a mere boy could ever replace you! Even a perfect splendid wonderful one. ☺

Poetess: He would be hopeless at picking outfits for you.

AmazonGrrrl!: And with the poetry? Not so much. Besides, if all we had were boys, who would listen to us talk about them? ;)

Poetess: Ooo! Speaking of poetry, I want to send you one I wrote last night when I got home.

AmazonGrrrl!: Is it about Nick? Already?

Poetess: No no no. I think you'll actually like this one.

AmazonGrrrl!: I liked that one about the colors of love! I've decided I want my love to be yellow.

Poetess: Like sunshine and daffodils and smiley faces, right?

AmazonGrrrl!: Precisely! ☺ Thank you, miss poetess.

Poetess: I imagine it will be. Anyway, I'll sign off and send this one to you. And I'll see you in school tomorrow, if your dad doesn't change his mind about Maine between now and then . . .

AmazonGrrrl!: Stop saying that! You'll give him ideas! Don't worry. We're all going to live happily ever after, you'll see.

Poetess: No objections here! ☺

AmazonGrrrl!: *hugs*

Poetess: *hugs* indeed.

Revision of an Ode

Dmitri
you say
there are stars
shining brightly from my eyes.
they are lasers
blazing down walls

Dmitri
you say
there are nightingales
singing softly in my voice.
do you not hear the dragons?
the thunder rolling when I roar?

Dmitri
you say
there is moonlight
glowing all around me.
I say
"Really? Thanks."
hitch a ride on a comet
and fly

ATHENWOOD PRODUCES A STAR!

BY SHARON BANTER

A report has come in that Hermia Jackson, whom some of you may remember as the very personable tree in last semester's Athenwood High School fall production, has been offered an extremely prestigious summer internship with the traveling tour of *The Faeries' Quarrel*, an interactive theater experience now playing in New York City to sold-out audiences.

Apparently one of the stars of the show, Tanya Moon, is a distant cousin of our own woodshop and sculpture teacher Ms. Polly Mason. Using these connections and her own starry personality, Hermia Jackson won the position and will be traveling with the show all summer. (Rumor has it that our theater's lighting designer, Alex Sanders, may be accompanying them as a technical intern as well.) Congratulations, Hermia!

ROMEO AND JULIO?

BY CHRISSY CANTON

Athenwood High School's spring production this year, a "truly Shakespearean" *Romeo and Juliet*, is that most terrifying of combinations: innovation and idiocy.

The director, Mr. Duke, seems to think that if an all-male cast was good enough for Shakespeare, it's good enough for Athenwood, although I personally doubt that Shakespeare ever had to deal with the likes of Athenwood's football team.

My concerns about this plan were confirmed in the opening minutes, when the prologue was delivered by Rob Taylor in a fit of starts and bursts, with pauses in all the oddest places. It was almost as if he had no idea what he was actually saying, which is apparently a common problem for him, if you ask any girl who has had the unfortunate experience of dating him.

The disaster level mounted as the play began with a scene of insults and brawling, much of which sounded suspiciously un-Shakespearean to *me*. We were soon treated to the spectacle of Peter Quincey as Tybalt, Juliet's hostile, attack-prone cousin. Quite frankly, Pete Quincey's acting ability is much like his ability to call a girl back: intermittent at best, and always startling when it does reveal itself. Rob Taylor performs double-duty, reappearing as the Nurse in some of the more (unintentionally) hilarious moments of the night. Watching the other actors try to interact with him as he stuck close to the edges of the stage and hid behind curtains was truly a sight to behold. And I can't even begin to TALK about Leo Sung and his fairly radical line interpretations.

However, there were a few shining moments in this chaotic spectacle, most notably our hunky quarterback Nick Weaver's surprisingly dreamy performance as Romeo. In what was perhaps the *only* wise decision affiliated with this production, Mr. Duke opted at the last minute to sub in Helena Naples as Juliet, instead of his original choice, Frank Flutie. Frank, meanwhile, was switched to take over the available role of Mercutio, mysteriously vacated by Dmitri Gilbert a week before opening. (And I have to say, Frank gave a vigorous, if slightly shrill, performance, perhaps motivated by relief at having escaped the role [and costumes] of the heroine.)

In any case, as all of you would know if Miss Phillips

would just let me write a gossip column already, Nick Weaver and Helena Naples are now AN ITEM (oo la la!) despite their troubled history (if you want to know more, write a letter to your editor! Demand a gossip column!). The magical glow of newfound love that surrounds their performance is almost *TOO* realistic, but you can't help rooting for these crazy kids anyhow. Nick, who tends toward grand gestures and exuberant posturing in most of his other scenes, manages to convey a compelling and utterly believable sense of his affection for Juliet in every moment he's on stage with her. Helena, for her part, gives her best performance yet, and speaking as someone who has gym with her and who frequently is forced to overhear many of her personal conversations, I've never seen her this excited about someone. Luckily they both die in the end (onstage), or we'd have to lynch them for being so sickeningly cute.

Lastly, there was one other notable and surprising performance: Tom O'Kinter, a quiet but capable defense player for the football team, is alarmingly adorable as Friar Lawrence. Someone tell that boy that priests aren't supposed to be so hot! And girls, *I* hear that his girlfriend DUMPED him AT the prom last week, so now he's single single single! I'd tell you all to go for him, except I fully intend to get there first.

So Tom and Nick, feel free to abandon football for theater, if the acting bug has got you now. But as for the rest of these guys? Don't give up your day jobs. And Mr. Duke, please seriously consider a musical for next year. I mean, who doesn't love Andrew Lloyd Webber?

(Oh, yeah, and Miss Phillips wants me to mention that the lights and set and costumes and stuff were pretty good, too.)

POET'S CORNER

Treachery, Thy Name Is . . .
by Dmitri Gilbert

O flummoxing fickleness!
O anguished despair!
O wanton ways!
O woman!

She cannot be trusted.
She will cause you woe.
She'll leave you for another.
She is woman, O!

Nobody knows the depths of
        my pain.
Nobody sees the tragic insides.
They're callous and heartless
        and cold
And utterly woman, besides.

So rip out my heart if you must
But don't expect to see me again.
I'll keep my sorrow hidden away.
And hide myself from my fellow
        man.

Terrible, tragic, thunderous agony
How could you leave me, I cry!
I am wounded to my soul, to my
        weary war-torn soul
I shall crawl away to die, die, die,
        die, die.

So this is your last chance.
E-mail me if you want me to take
        you back.
And I'll think about it.